"I want to hold you and kiss you and not stop," Zack said.

"Do you know what I'm saying? You're special to me, and I don't think you realize it."

"Please," she whispered, her eyes filled with tears. "I can't handle this."

"Ask me anyth
to tell you how I
you were in my
want to touch you
How I want to he
me not to stop? H—— —— —— know each other for years and never feel the way I do. If I didn't think you felt the same way, I wouldn't be saying this."

"Zack, it's no good. Please don't say any more." Her voice sounded tinny in her ears. The things he said were true. She did want to kiss him, to be with him, but she'd learned a hard lesson in her life—don't wish for things that might come true, heartache is bound to follow.

"All right, then," he murmured. "How about a hug for a friend?"

Her mind warned her not to go into his waiting arms, not to react to his boyish grin, not to want. She was so certain she could resist him, but in the instant he clasped her to him and grazed the soft skin of her cheek with his lips, she knew it was too late.

"Hannah, we're destined to be more than friends. . . ."

WHAT ARE *LOVESWEPT* ROMANCES?

They are stories of true romance and touching emotion. We believe those two very important ingredients are constants in our highly sensual and very believable stories in the *LOVESWEPT* line. Our goal is to give you, the reader, stories of consistently high quality that may sometimes make you laugh, sometimes make you cry, but are always fresh and creative and contain many delightful surprises within their pages.

Most romance fans read an enormous number of books. Those they truly love, they keep. Others may be traded with friends and soon forgotten. We hope that each *LOVESWEPT* romance will be a treasure—a "keeper." We will always try to publish

LOVE STORIES YOU'LL NEVER FORGET
BY AUTHORS YOU'LL ALWAYS REMEMBER

The Editors

LOVESWEPT® • 388

Doris Parmett
Heartthrob

BANTAM BOOKS
NEW YORK • TORONTO • LONDON • SYDNEY • AUCKLAND

HEARTTHROB

A Bantam Book / March 1990

Published simultaneously in the United States and Canada

PRINTED IN THE UNITED STATES OF AMERICA

O   0 9 8 7 6 5 4 3 2 1

To my friends,
Alice and David Jurist,
for more reasons
than I can list.
Thanks.

Much appreciation
to television producers
Scott Rokosny
and
David Garb
for their technical
assistance.

One

"My luck!"

Director Zachary Matthews strode into the control room. He thumped a script against his thigh with a murderous thwack, then flung it onto the nearest chair, clamped on his headset, and glared at the preview monitor.

"Camera One!" he said into his mike. "Why wasn't that camera bubble balanced before? Your picture's shaky."

Slouched in a seat next to him, audio engineer Scott Rosser sat up, obviously annoyed at his friend's uncharacteristic rudeness. "Quit taking it out on Babs."

Everybody in the television studio knew about the shouting match Zack and station owner Morris Winger had had following that morning's preproduction meeting. The row had rivaled any on a nighttime soap opera.

And all because of Morris's niece Hannah Morgan.

On the set below, Babs McCauley jumped to attention, leveling the camera to an imaginary horizon line. Zack hooked his thumbs into his back pockets. "That's good. Lock it." A few seconds later he added, "Sorry I blew up at you, kid. You're doing fine."

"If you ask me, it's your attitude," Scott muttered.

"What's wrong with my attitude?" Zack bellowed. "I'm the soul of nice."

"Maybe before," Scott said. "Not now. By the way, Hannah's already at the studio."

"Terrific!" Zack threw up his hands.

"Look at the bright side," Scott said. "She might fall in love with you. They say togetherness breeds . . . something."

"Are you deliberately provoking me?" Zack asked.

Scott tossed him an orange lollipop. Scott was addicted to the sweet, and had color-coded the days of the week with them. Thursday was orange.

Zack unwrapped the candy. "Why can't I have grape?"

Scott shook his head. "Grape's Tuesday. Don't look a gift horse in the mouth. I hate an ungrateful moocher." He adjusted the audio level as the guests on the set said a few words for the voice check, then went on. "I'm just trying to help you see this from a better perspective. Take a word of advice from one who's cooled his heels on the unemployment line a few times. When Hannah Morgan comes in here, behave."

"Can you give me one good reason why I should be saddled with her? There are at least ten worthy candidates I'd hire first."

"Ah, but you didn't hire her, and that's exactly my point."

"You didn't read her resumé. I did. It wasn't hard to memorize. Hannah Morgan: Attended college for one semester. Spent two months arranging silk flowers for a specialty store. Four months as a receptionist for an advertising agency. In a six-month span of time she was a hostess at an automobile show and worked in a travel agency. That was a year ago. Heaven forbid she should stick to something and go to school for a degree in communications like the rest of us. You know my crazy schedule. I haven't come up for air in months."

"Did you mention that to Morris?"

"I did." Zack massaged the knot at the back of his neck, an aching reminder of having worked in the editing suite until three in the morning.

"What did he say?"

Zack shrugged. "The usual complimentary garbage." In fact, he preferred not to repeat what Morris had said. His leprechaun face had wrinkled into a cajoling grin, right before he launched into his reasons for having Zack train Hannah, making Zack sound about as interesting as fungus mildewing a cellar.

"You're the perfect choice," Morris had told him. "You're here day and night, which makes you ideal. You're probably celibate, which is fine, since I don't want you making a play for her. She's here to learn. I've arranged her schedule to coincide with yours. There's one thing, though. She's got to be home by six."

With that insulting and depressing news, Morris

had pushed away from his desk and wended his ample girth out of the room and down the hall, whistling.

Scott broke into Zack's gloomy thoughts. "Don't blow this job. You're producing and directing. Except for this you've got a free rein."

Zack feigned indifference. "Think of the bright side. It'll give you a chance to move up."

Scott emphatically shook his head, tousling his thick thatch of red hair. A tiny diamond twinkled in his right earlobe.

"No thanks. You're the workaholic, not me. There are twenty-four hours in a day, half of which are meant to be spent enjoying the opposite sex. By the way, how are you doing in *that* department?"

The truth was, Zack wasn't doing anything in *that* department. His divorce had cured him of commitments; concern over disease had put a lid on casual sex.

All smiles, Morris entered the booth, disregarding the *On Air* light. "Zack, meet my favorite niece, Hannah Morgan. Hannah darlin'," he drawled, trotting out his native Georgia accent, "meet Zachary Matthews. Zack's most kindly offered to take you under his wing. Once you get the feel for the way we work, Zack'll find out what you're best suited for. I've already told him when you need to leave." He stared at Zack meaningfully, squeezed Hannah's arm, then excused himself and left.

Zack ignored Morris's syrupy affectation. He barely even heard him slide the door closed in back of him. He was too busy reacting to the punch in his solar plexus. Hannah Morgan wasn't what he'd expected.

He didn't want her to look as if she'd just stepped off the pages of a high-fashion magazine, in an outfit appropriate for high tea. He wanted her to look as he'd imagined, complete with funky clothes, frizzed hair, garish makeup, and a bored expression.

She wasn't like that at all.

Her eyes were the color of budding leaves, veiled by a sooty forest of impudently curling lashes. Thick nutmeg-brown hair shot through with copper high-lights tumbled about a lovely oval-shaped face. If she were a couple of inches taller, she could earn a hefty living as a model.

His preference in women didn't run to the skinny or the flat-chested. Hannah was neither. He was sorry her periwinkle-blue wool suit and pale laven-der blouse were not meant to flatter her stunning figure.

She extended her right hand. "I'm very pleased to meet you, Mr. Matthews."

As his hand closed around hers, he realized her skin was as soft and tantalizing as her voice. For a split second he allowed her fathomless eyes, her delicate perfume to mesmerize him. Then he re-minded himself of who she was and why she was there. He gave her hand a brief, hard shake. "Nice to meet you, too, Miss Morgan," he said flatly.

Hannah's heart was pounding hard as Zack re-leased her hand and stepped back. The instant she had seen him, a flash fire had exploded within her, fast and furious. She searched his eyes, enthralled and intimidated by the brief flare of hunger she glimpsed there. She seen that intense look before, and had learned to shy away from it. Only once had it affected her. And then she'd made the biggest mistake of her life.

"I appreciate your taking me on," she murmured, tucking her hand into her skirt pocket. He didn't respond, and for a moment she allowed herself to study him. Like the other man in the control room, he was casually dressed in a cotton shirt and jeans. He was remarkably handsome, and she guessed he was in his early thirties. He had dark eyes with lashes as black as his ebony hair. Tall and lean, he had a natural commanding presence, and she knew she was looking at a man who set carefully planned goals—and reached them.

"We're about to start a show, Miss Morgan," he said coolly. "Find a seat and keep out of the way."

Bewildered, Hannah stared at him. Only a fool would miss his implication or the moment of un-guarded irritation. And, she realized with stunning clarity, that he was angry with himself too. Why?

She lifted her chin, gazing directly into his eyes. "Thanks to you, I hope to learn this business, Mr. Matthews."

So what did she expect? she asked herself. A smile instead of a grunt? Compassion in a man's world? Where would she be without her Uncle Morris? Philosophically, she was against nepotism. But philosophical truths and personal opinions against nepotism didn't pay the rent. Her actions were dictated by an overriding need to provide a home for herself and her infant daughter. There was no husband to share her burden. Life wasn't fair. She ought to know. She could write a book on the subject.

Submerging her painful memories, she flipped back the cover of the yellow legal pad, poised to begin.

Zack half-convinced himself he'd spoken so brusquely to her to test her, to see her reaction. With a mixture of admiration and annoyance, he grudgingly respected her for not flinching. She radiated determination from the tip of her shiny hair to her toes.

He turned to face the monitors and spoke into his mike. "Countdown starting. Okay. Good. We're up to speed. Audio up." He could say the standard litany in his sleep. In his peripheral vision he saw Hannah begin to write on her pad. Was she going to copy down everything he said?

"Ready music . . . and music up on three. Graphics in. Change it. Dissolve to camera one. Music down . . . and go." Babs, using a prearranged hand signal, cued Madge Evans, the hostess for the daily talk show.

Madge welcomed Paxton, New Jersey's colorful septuagenarian librarian, the venerable Agnes Loring. Using the preview and program monitors, Zack maintained the flow with automatic precision, knowing exactly what he wanted.

The tape counter tracked the time. Fifteen minutes later, he cued up a commercial and rocked back on the balls of his feet. Why had Hannah changed jobs so often? he wondered. And where had she worked the past year? He was unable to come up with an answer. The countdown began. Bob Hope made his appearance.

As Zack pinched the bridge of his nose, he sensed her gaze on him. He turned around. Their eyes met, electric currents sparking like jolts of lightning.

"Are you finding this interesting?" he asked, unreasonably irritated that after his big blowup with Morris, he found her fascinating.

"Oh, yes," she said.

"As interesting as arranging silk flowers? Or hostessing a car show? Or working in a travel agency? I didn't leave anything out, did I?"

Hannah's breath caught in her throat. Scott coughed. Zack's attention never wavered.

She rose. If only her resumé weren't such a paltry joke, she thought. She should have made up something to hide the gaps for last year. "You've about covered it."

"Well, let's hope you find this sustains your interest."

Hannah inwardly seethed. She lowered her eyes until she was back in control, then looked up at Zack. "Part of that depends on how good a teacher you are, doesn't it?" she said, her eyes bright, her tone innocent.

His mouth quirked. "Your uncle claims I'm the best."

"My uncle," she murmured, forcing gratitude into her voice, "is usually right."

"Your uncle"—he stressed the word—"pulled rank."

So that was it, she mused. That was why he resented her. Morris had given him no say in the matter. She'd been crammed down his throat. "I had no idea you were coerced. I'll try not to make a nuisance of myself with too many questions."

She needed this man; he held the key to her future. She sensed he could be generous if he chose to . . . and that he would not be generous with her. She squared her shoulders. In the past two years she'd dealt with tougher situations. *Too bad, Mr.*

Matthews, she told him silently. *I'm staying whether you approve of me or not.* She had to. She was desperate.

The taping resumed, and Zack chalked Round One up to her. She was smart. Cool. Diplomatic. Yes, she'd apologized for the way she'd been sent to him. But she hadn't offered to quit because of it. He had the feeling she could diffuse an impending war if she chose. She'd quietly agreed with his conclusions, as if it were the most natural thing in the world for her to be treated rudely.

He sensed she could become a bigger problem if he allowed her to creep under his skin. If eyes were the mirror of one's soul, he sure hoped no one looked into his. The last time he'd felt such a rush for a woman, he'd made a mistake that had taken five long years to unravel. He ran his hand across the back of his neck.

As the half-hour show drew to a close, Zack wrapped it up. He called for music to run underneath the credits. He wondered if Hannah danced. His hands could probably span her tiny waist. As quickly as the thought wormed its way into his consciousness, he squelched it.

The picture faded from the screen. Zack flipped a switch, allowing his voice to be audible on the set. "Agnes, you're a honey. Nice job, guys." Babs McCauley, rolling her camera off to the side, glanced up and stuck out her tongue, knowing he'd see it on the monitor.

Forgetting his audience, Zack chuckled. "Sorry, honey. Good job, Camera Person. Babs, be nice to me and I won't tell anyone you've got the hots for Scott."

Scott jabbed his arm. He and Babs fought good-naturedly and constantly. Must be love, Zack mused, removing his headset. It wasn't in the stars for him, though. He doubted he'd ever feel that way again.

Flexing cramped muscles, he ran his fingers through his hair, then glanced at Hannah. She was gazing curiously at him. He wondered if she'd been shocked to hear him laugh.

"Coffee?" he asked. "We've got time before the next taping begins."

She nodded and followed him out into the hall-way. The wide space served several purposes. Desks, reserved for scheduling, scriptwriting, contacting future talent, and many other functions, were littered with papers and remnants of hastily consumed cups of coffee. On one desk was a basket of assorted bagels and a tub of cream cheese, donated daily by Marty, one of the ad salesmen, who owned a bagel franchise on the side. A large scheduling board covered half of one wall.

Dolores Farley, the mayor's wife and the "talent" for the next taping, entered the hall hanging onto Madge's arm. Madge wore a pained expression. Zack suppressed a grin. Dolores did that to people.

Nodding to the women, he led Hannah to the table that held the coffee urn. Pouring hot liquid into a Styrofoam cup, he tried to remember how much coffee he'd drunk that morning. Five was his usual limit. At six his nerves jangled. He sipped the coffee and watched as Hannah half-filled a cup with cold milk.

"You don't drink coffee?" he asked.

She as surprised at the personal question. "No."

"Why? Does it keep you up at night?"

No, she answered silently, *it's not good for a nursing mother.* Right then she would have died for the cup of coffee he was drinking, though. "Caffeine's not good for the system."

"What about decaf?"

"There isn't any." He hadn't noticed it before, but she was right. He'd have to see about ordering some for her.

Lounging against the wall, Zack found himself studying her with the eye of a director deciding on a camera shot. His gaze lingered on her mouth. There was a drop of milk at one corner. Had he known her better he might have reached for a napkin to blot it. Had they been lovers he would have kissed it away. The thought stunned him. What would Morris say if he knew? He moved his gaze on to her hair, watching the light dance in it.

Taking another fortifying sip of coffee, he wondered why he was even mildly interested in understanding his fascination with her. She was quite young, probably ten years his junior. And she certainly was too short by his standards. He liked women whose eyes were level with his.

So what was it? Her clean, just-bathed-and-powdered scent? Or that she was unfazed by his less-than-gracious manner? Or that her serenity wove a web of memories in his mind? She was a world apart from his ex-wife. Maybe that was her appeal. There was a wistful quality about her, yet he also sensed a steely determination. It was a unique combination.

Madge paused near the table, smiling politely at Hannah. Zack quickly made the introductions, then listened while Madge filled him in on the latest problem.

"Dolores Farley's brought another guest. You know our mayor's wife. Hannah, you're lucky you're not interviewing her. She organizes everything to her best advantage. Today she's touting her husband's pet project. Sorry to spring this on you at the last minute, Zack. Oh, and she has two blank tapes. Is it okay?"

Zack moved aside for a tour group. With the way his luck was running that day, he thought, Dolores's manipulations were minor.

"No problem. Give them to Scott. He'll see they're dubbed." Madge nodded and turned her attention to Hannah, scrutinizing her with professional interest. They chatted a while, then Madge said to Zack, "You ought to put Hannah in front of the camera instead of behind it. We've got enough camera operators."

"I'd be a bundle of nerves if I had to do what you do, Madge," Hannah said. "I don't know how you do it. All that timing and making sure the talents let each other speak." Morris had told her Madge was one of the best interviewers in the business. At least once a year she turned down jobs with the networks.

"You've got a fabulous speaking voice," Madge said. She turned to Zack. "She could be trained. And that face. Don't listen to her. Put her in front of the camera. Trust me. I know what I'm talking about. Try her on a one-minute segment."

Zack looked hard at Madge. Her voice was strained, as if she had a bad sore throat, and he wondered why she was pushing Hannah all of a sudden. She'd just met her, knew nothing about her. "Are you thinking of leaving us?" he asked. "Is something up?"

She looked past his shoulder to Morris, who was walking toward them. "Don't be silly. I simply stated my opinion. In some circles it's worth a lot."

"Am I interrupting?" Morris asked, linking hands with Hannah.

"Morris," Madge said, "I was just telling Zack I think Hannah can do more good for WBC in front of the camera than behind it. What do you think? A voice-over to start with, and then a short segment?"

"Don't give him any ideas," Hannah pleaded. She had no notion what a "voice-over" was, or a "short segment." This was fantasy talk, idle chatter she wasn't going to allow herself to think about. First she had to crawl; then she'd learn to walk. But what a nice compliment!

Morris put an arm around her shoulders, giving her a quick squeeze. "Darlin' girl, Madge never says things she doesn't mean, not when your future is so important. I always say opportunity's right around the corner. You never know. Maybe one day Zack'll give you the chance to do a voice-over or go out on location to film a spot."

"You're talking in riddles," Hannah said. "What's a voice-over?"

Zack answered. "Suppose the station wanted to advertise a coming show. We'd show shots to promote it. The offscreen voice you hear describing it is the voice-over."

"See, darlin', there's nothing to it. It's a good way to get experience." Morris excused himself and strolled over to the tour group to welcome them. Zack filed the suggestion away for future use. He'd have to clear up Hannah's misimpression that he controlled her career. Morris did. Still, Morris rarely proposed anything on the spur of the moment, and Madge was acting mysterious. Why?

The next taping went like a breeze—if you liked one-sided conversations. Madge almost lost control. If she had been less experienced she would have. Each time she asked Dolores's uninvited guest a question, Dolores answered out of camera range. On top of that, Dolores's long hair kept brushing against her mike, making it sound as if it were raining on the set. Scott threw up his hands. Zack called for a wide shot and left it there.

"Is it always like this?" Hannah asked during a commercial.

"It was pretty bad," he said. "We could reshoot it, but it would back up the rest of the schedule. I doubt if the others could come back. We had a hard time getting them together today."

Hannah wrote steadily, filling up page after page of notes. A half an hour later Zack cued up the wrap and stalked out of the control room, heading for his sixth cup of coffee. Thinking of Hannah, he scalded his tongue. He cursed and blew on the hot liquid. As he watched, he saw her emerge from the control room with Scott. His head was bent close to hers as he intently answered a question. Scott seemed taken with her too, Zack thought.

He quickly finished his coffee and crushed the empty cup, tossing it into the wastepaper basket. How would Miss Calmness handle Dolores? he wondered. No doubt she'd have her eating out of her hand, as she did Scott. She walked over to the table and poured another half cup of milk.

"Why do you want to learn the business?" he asked suddenly. Something about her didn't add up. She didn't seem the type to flit from job to job. She seemed . . . reliable.

Startled by his question, Hannah took a moment to swallow some milk before answering. Zack had been watching her and waiting to pounce. It was bad enough she had to keep reminding herself to drink her milk. Being put under a microscope by him made it worse.

"I'm more than willing to go the extra mile," she said. "Whatever you want me to do, I'll do."

"Do you always answer a question without giving away information? Why television?"

She drank the last of the milk. "Why not? It's a good field. There's opportunity in it—"

"Especially," he cut in, "if you're family. Never mind. I'm beating a dead horse, and it's none of my business."

She carefully kept all trace of emotion from her voice. "Thank you for respecting my privacy."

Dammit! he thought. She'd done it to him again. Somewhere she'd perfected the art of the subtle put-down. "If you're serious about learning, I wouldn't count on leaving at six every night. We work crazy hours, often ten or twelve a day. It's not going to leave you much time for a social life. Are you married?"

She colored and she licked her lips. "No."

"Going with anyone?"

She bristled. "Is this part of your interview?"

He bristled right back. At last he'd gotten a rise out of her. "What interview? The only reason I'm asking is because if you are, it's going to put a crimp in your plans. Regardless of your relationship with Morris, I have to work with you. I won't put up with anyone who can't go the pace."

Hannah struggled to rein in her newly released temper. Since she'd been living alone, she met any injustice with an instant reaction. If she closed her eyes, she could hear her ex-husband accusing her of having no skills. Skills she hadn't had time to gain because she'd quit school to marry him, then had followed him from place to place. The best she'd landed were temporary jobs.

"I assure you," she said coolly, "that I have no wish to arrange silk flowers all my life, any more than you do."

The air crackled between them as messages zinged back and forth.

Why do you hate me?

I don't need complications in my life.

I won't be.

Wanna bet?

She tried again—for her daughter's sake. "Mr. Matthews, I'm truly sorry I've been foisted on you. It's clear you'd like to tell me where to get off and you think you can't because of my uncle."

"You're wrong," he said bluntly. Ever since he'd set eyes on her she'd been causing his emotions to swing, as if he were an adolescent with galloping hormones.

"I don't approve of unearned nepotism," he went on. "We have several fine candidates with training who deserve any job that opens up. Many have worked after school without compensation or for very low pay, just to get a break. Incidentally, your Uncle

Morris has been telling us there's no money in the budget to hire new people."

They moved apart, each wondering how far to go.

"You've made your point," Hannah said. "Now let me make mine. I'm sorry about all the more qualified people you'd hire over me. It might surprise you to know I agree with you. But I have my reasons for wanting to succeed. For both our sakes, I'd prefer to get along with you. You don't have to like me. I'm not trying to win a popularity contest with you, but I wish you'd give me a chance. In the end it's to your advantage."

He leaned closer, irked by her implication. "You'd better rethink your wishes. Until you arrived I was doing just fine. I spend what precious little spare time I have putting together a documentary that's important to me. Now I have a shadow I don't want. A shadow who knows nothing, who's going to cut into that time. I'm also expected to teach you the ropes while trying to do my job. On top of that I've been told you have to leave for home before the rest of us, when it's a damned sight more convenient for me not to interrupt my day. The least you could do is to stay later so I can explain things to you. Did you really expect to win brownie points with me?"

No one could accuse him of unnecessary chitchat, she thought, forcing herself to hold his gaze. His biting remarks cut to the quick. It took every bit of her control to swallow the lump in her throat. His reasons for resenting her made sense. Still, she couldn't deny his potent effect on her. He was a man who could turn her insides to jelly when he smiled, who was as good-looking as a movie star, and whom she couldn't tell anything about herself. Behind his handsome, intriguing face could be the same kind of man she'd married. Ambitious. A climber. A user.

She'd made Morris promise not to reveal anything about her daughter. She'd tell people when she was ready, she'd said, only agreeing to the job when he'd promised. Morris, unmarried all his life, and her sister Alexandra, two years older than she and single, couldn't possibly understand her feelings. They'd never walked in her shoes. She was determined to keep her private life hidden—at least until she'd proven herself.

She wondered what Zack's reaction would be if he knew about Sarah. He was a man, and many men scoffed at mothers in the workplace, women who put family considerations on an equal par with their jobs.

She wished she were home nursing her baby, not standing there trying to fight back tears. She loved holding Sarah in her arms with the infant's sweet rosebud mouth pressed to her nipple. Thinking of her daughter, she gained control.

But not enough to hide the droop of her shoulders, or her weary sigh. She turned away from Zack to avoid giving him the satisfaction of seeing her make a fool of herself.

Zack was sorry the minute he finished his tirade. He'd seen her bottom lip quiver. He'd pushed her too far. For the first time he was disgusted with himself. He'd taken his anger at Morris out on her. He touched her shoulder. She jumped.

Irritation drained from him. "Is something wrong?"

"No, of course not."

"I didn't mean to upset you. I'm sure you'll do fine."

Stunned by his sudden reversal, Hannah slowly turned to face him. The beginnings of a fragile trust sank in, warming her insides with tentative hope.

"Wait here a minute," he said. He went into his office and returned with a book. "One of the students left this. She's in Europe for a semester as an exchange student. I'm sure she won't mind if you borrow it. Read the first couple of chapters. Familiarize yourself with the lingo and some of the basics. We'll go over it tomorrow. Then get a good night's sleep. You'll need it. Be here at eight-thirty. We have a daily preproduction meeting then."

She scooped up her coat, slinging it over her arm. "Mr. Matthews?"

"You might as well call me Zack."

She smiled. "You did say eight-thirty?"

"Promptly."

She nodded, then glanced at Scott. "Thanks for your kindness."

"Anytime, Hannah," Scott said.

The remark wasn't lost on Zack, and he glared at Scott as Hannah walked away. Then he looked after her, his gaze fixing on her gently swaying hips. She paused at the door to toss a remark over her shoulder. She sounded surprisingly young and carefree.

"Better watch that coffee, Scott. Caffeine can make a person grouchy."

Scott howled and cuffed Zack on the back as she went out the door. "Hot damn, but she's cute. I'll take her off your hands if you want. After all, I know just as much as you."

Zack balled his fists. He could rapidly grow to hate Scott. "She's not your responsibility, she's mine."

"Well, I'll be damned," Scott said. "If the old Heart-throb hasn't finally risen to the bait on the home turf. You're going to break a lot of hearts, pal. You do know the women here have a pool going, betting on when and if you ever date someone who works at WBC."

Zack grinned sheepishly. He knew. "Knock it off. Besides, Hannah's just a kid."

Scott laughed. "Buddy, if she's just a kid, you're blind. She's some kind of woman."

When Zack finally left the studio, the moon had bathed the parking lot with silvery light. He felt a loneliness engulf him, the type of which he'd never known. Much later, after eating a tasteless TV dinner and rewriting a script, he lay in bed with his hands linked behind his neck, staring out at the sky. He wasn't blind. Hannah *was* some kind of woman.

His thoughts weren't of Scott or Morris or the next day's hectic schedule. They were of a Dresden-like beauty, with glistening hair and wondrous peridot eyes, who adroitly managed to avoid answering any personal questions, while delivering a one-two punch. There certainly was more to her than met the eye.

The reporter in him intended to find out.

The man in him wondered how Hannah's hair would look with moonbeams gathered in its silken strands.

Two

Hannah stretched her arms over her head, the term paper she'd typed for Steven Smith completed. The extra income wouldn't be much, but it gave her confidence. She hadn't told Morris or Alexandra she did typing and light sewing, and had spoken to a local florist about making silk-flower arrangements at home. The shop owner was only too delighted to hire her for piecework.

Though well-meaning, Morris and Alex would scold her for the long hours she put in. "You're a mother!" Alex would exclaim, as if that meant she should be resting whenever Sarah did. She was grateful that Steven was all thumbs with a keyboard and that his mother was too busy commuting to New York City to have any energy left to sew. Mrs. Smith had even told her friends about Hannah's meticulous work.

Determined to prove to Zack that she wasn't a mental toad, she spent a good part of the evening studying the chapters he'd assigned her, only putting the textbook down when the words began to blur on the page. Still, she was on too much of an adrenaline high to sleep, so she wandered the neat Cape Cod house creating jobs.

She did the laundry, washed and scrubbed the kitchen floor, and folded baby clothes. The clothes went into the chest of drawers she'd bought secondhand and proudly painted yellow, then decorated with stenciled Pennsylvania Dutch flowers.

She rechecked the list of emergency phone numbers, making certain hers and the pediatrician's were double-underlined in red. She showered and shampooed her hair, dried it, then tried out different styles, hoping to make herself look older and more accomplished. At one in the morning she slipped between the violet-scented sheets and lay awake thinking about her new job . . . and Zack.

As if Sarah sensed this was the beginning of a new routine, the infant spent a fretful night. Hannah checked her temperature twice, and hovered over the crib countless times monitoring her breathing. To Hannah, Sarah was the most perfect baby ever. She'd do anything for her; all of her actions were motivated by an overwhelming need to provide a good life for her daughter. When Morris had offered her a career, not just a temporary job, she'd jumped at the chance. It had been scary moving away from California on pure hope. She'd known her luck was changing, though, when her new next-door neighbor, Phyllis Fischer, agreed to take care of Sarah during the day.

In the morning Hannah dragged herself out of bed

to nurse Sarah. She'd slept a total of two uninterrupted hours. She splashed cold water on her face and bathed her eyes. When it was time for her to leave, Sarah's tiny mouth quivered and huge tears overflowed her round blue-green eyes, spiking her lashes like sentinels of accusation. Her tiny fingers clasped her mother's.

"Great." Hannah sniffled, consumed with guilt. She kissed the downy blond curls and handed Sarah to Phyllis. "This is supposed to be the first day of the rest of my life."

"Wait until Sarah's first day of school," the older woman said. "Then you'll know what separation is."

Hannah let Phyllis shoo her out the door. She slid behind the wheel of her car, besieged with regret, and turned the key. The engine coughed, caught, then stalled. Grimacing, she pressed the accelerator to the floor and gave the key a vicious twist. The car roared, then stalled again. The distinct aroma of gasoline filled the air.

Great, she thought, resting her forehead on the wheel. She'd flooded the engine. She'd wait a few minutes, get herself under control, then try again. She would not let her dampened spirits weigh her down. Thanks to Morris—and Zack—tomorrow was bright. And today . . . today she'd make it, with or without sleep.

Trusting she'd given the engine enough time, she carefully turned the key. The car started just fine, and she pulled out into the street. Glancing at her watch, though, she saw she was going to be late. Anxiety rose in her, and she pressed harder on the gas.

Two minutes later a policeman pulled her over and ticketed her for driving five miles an hour over the speed limit in a residential area. Fighting tears, she continued on to the studio, parked, and bolted into the building. She sprinted down the long corridor, her shoulder bag bouncing against her hip.

Everyone Scott had pointed out to her the previous day was now in the staff room. Zack was leading the meeting, and paused in the middle of a sentence as she raced in. Ten pairs of eyes focused on her. She was twenty minutes late. She avoided Zack's piercing gaze.

"So . . ." Zack said, watching her with increasing delight. Was it the promise of spring that made his blood heat? Or was it the sight of her? She was as colorful as a butterfly. A warm flush tinged her cheeks, matching her lips.

Her expressive eyes sparkled in that amazing shade he knew he'd never tire of seeing. Tiny tendrils of hair wisped over her forehead, framing her perfectly oval-shaped face. He'd spent a lot of time the night before thinking about the shape of her lips. Correction, he mused. He'd spent a lot of time thinking about the taste of her lips.

His appreciative gaze traveled downward to the swell of her breasts, hidden primly beneath a peach-colored jacket. She was a diminutive young woman in the fullness of her beauty. She was also blushing furiously.

Nearly suffocating with embarrassment, Hannah nodded briefly to Scott and Madge, then wedged past the others at the table to the only empty seat in the room. Right beside Zack.

She swallowed past the lump in her throat and willed herself to meet his gaze. "I'm sorry, Zack. The engine flooded."

"Cars are tricky machines," he said with mock seriousness. He flung his arm out to pull out the chair next to him. She bumped her wrist on the back of the chair, jarring her arm and sending the contents of her purse scattering onto the floor—most of which rolled beneath Zack's chair.

Hannah gasped and ducked. On hands and knees she hurriedly began to scoop up her possessions. Zack called a short break. Everyone headed out the door for coffee and bagels.

Horrified, Hannah saw a pink pacifier resting atop Zack's right shoe. Even as she prayed he wouldn't move, he bent down to help. And almost choked!

He hooked the tip of his index finger through the plastic handle, clearly amazed as the strains of a lullaby came from its base. "Yours?" he whispered, wiggling the pacifier like a ticking metronome. She shook her head.

"Boyfriend?" Hannah groaned. His eyes crinkled at the corners. "I suppose it's a good way to introduce a child to music. Tell me, does this come in Beethoven's Fifth or a Moody Blues?"

Hannah was getting the idea that a playful Zack was harder to deal with than a businesslike Zack. Humor emphasized his handsomeness, lighting up his eyes and curving his mouth into an enchanting smile. Their faces were so close they exchanged breaths.

"So . . ." he said, "you baby-sit." Question. Statement. He waited.

"Yes," she said in a strangled voice.

"Lucky baby," he murmured, his gaze focusing on her lips.

She reached for the pacifier with trembling fingers. All of her carefully laid plans . . .

"What the . . . ?" His grin disappeared. On his knees, too, he steadied her quaking shoulders, then slid his hands up her neck to cup her chin, his eyes searching her face. "I was only joking. Hey, it's okay," he said reassuringly.

"Please," she whispered shakily, drawing away from the comfort he offered. She wanted to dig a hole and crawl in rather than let him see her this way. "They're coming back." This was not the time to tell him about Sarah.

She still carried painful memories of her husband's chauvinistic attitude. Larry had poked fun at women who attempted to balance a career and a home, especially those competing in his chosen field: television. Alexandra and Morris kept trying to convince her Larry's meanness stemmed from insecurity. Maybe, but she knew Larry's opinion wasn't unique. After all she'd been through, she had to keep her public and private life separate, for Sarah's sake. At least until she felt secure in her job.

When she and the others were seated, Madge tried to ease her embarrassment. "Let me tell you about my first day in front of the camera, Hannah. I dropped the script and was too nervous to pick it up."

"And she mixed up the names of the guests," Scott added helpfully.

"But lived to tell the tale," Madge said, coughing behind a tissue. "Welcome to the club, honey. First

days are hell, but the sun always rises in the morning, giving us a second chance." Hannah could have
kissed her.

Zack leaned down to speak in her ear. "Are you all
right?" he asked in a low, worried tone.

She nodded. "Fine. I'm sorry. Madge was right.
First-day jitters." She as aware of the clean, tangy
scent of his lotion. He was dressed in a dark business suit, white shirt, red print tie. She was certain
she looked a disheveled mess after her horrible
experience.

"You look fine," he whispered. Awash with the
realization that he had correctly read her thoughts,
she pretended not to hear.

The room was too warm. Since giving birth, her
body reacted differently to heat. Heat, nerves, and
lack of sleep combined to make her drowsy. Her
eyelids drooped. She blinked awake and snuck a
glance at the others to make certain no one caught
her stifling a yawn into a tissue.

As the meeting continued, the voices droned in
her head. She barely heard the discussion. Zack
was sitting close, too close. The warmth from his
body seemed to seep into her, draining her of the
energy and will to sit erect. The urge to lean against
him was overpowering. She was crazy, she knew it.
Or else she was so tired she'd lost her perspective.
He was her nemesis; yet she was feeling as if he
were her dearest friend in the whole world, just
because he'd smiled at her and asked her if she was
all right.

"Unless anyone has something to add, that should
do it, folks." Zack stuffed his papers into his attaché
case. He rose, eager to end the preproduction meeting.

Madge gathered her file. "How are you coming with the documentary you plan on entering for the ACE Award?"

"Still plugging away. One of these days it'll be finished."

Madge paused near the door. "I expect to see your credits on network television. Don't forget us peons."

"Some peon," Zack scoffed. "As I recall, you've turned down some pretty lucrative offers." He nodded to the others as they left, then stopped Hannah, his hand on her arm. "Just a minute, please. I'd like a word with you, then we'll go over the chapters."

Hannah did her utmost to suppress a fresh attack of nerves. Here it comes, she thought. The chewing out for being late.

Gritting her teeth, she prepared for the worst. He knew she'd practically fallen asleep, not exactly giving the impression of a gung ho trainee. Still, what could he do to her? Nothing. Besides, she reminded herself grimly, she could always type, sew, and arrange flowers. It wouldn't be much of an income, but in time she might be able to branch out.

"Do you feel well?" Zack asked.

Startled, she looked up. He was gazing at her with a frown of worry, seeming genuinely concerned. "Yes, why do you ask?"

His gentle gaze touched her face. "Just wondered. I thought perhaps you aren't feeling well."

"Not feeling well. Not well," she repeated blankly.

"That's what I said. Well, do you?"

She was light-headed, giddy from lack of sleep and relief. Quite unexpectedly, she laughed, a lyrical, happy sound.

"Is something funny?" he snapped, his irritation with her rising unexpectedly. He'd spent far too much time dwelling on her as it was. Yesterday . . . last night . . . when he'd tossed and turned in bed. Even the Johnny Carson show had failed to interest him.

It wasn't his fault. He'd never seen eyes such an extraordinary shade as hers. This morning he'd considerately waited until the last possible moment to begin the meeting. And during it he'd worried about her, wondering why she looked so tired. And then she laughed at him!

"Am I amusing you?" he asked curtly.

Hannah spread her hands in a helpless gesture. They brushed against his broad chest, and she felt the reflexive leap of his strong muscles. "Forgive me, Zack. I steeled myself for a scolding. Which, by the way, you've every right to give me. Then you ask about my health. It was a surprise, that's all."

"I don't scold," he said soberly. "You don't have to be afraid of me."

He reminded her of a little boy. She peeked at him from beneath a fan of sooty lashes. "Not even a little?"

He grinned, amused and delighted to see her shift in mood. "Maybe a little," he admitted.

Hannah lifted her chin. Lack of sleep loosened her tongue. "No, you command the troops with those coal-black eyes, Mr. Matthews, and everybody jumps."

He chuckled. "As bad as that, huh?"

She bobbed her head. "Worse." She yawned, cupping her hand over her mouth. "Definitely. Do you know I was ticketed this morning? My first. The policeman wasn't impressed. He read me the riot act."

"Really." A smile tugged at his lips. "You don't look like a criminal to me." He lifted his hand, but somehow resisted the impulse to cup her chin and kiss the pout off her lips.

She grimaced. "Maybe not to you. *He* treated me as if I were a criminal. Anyway, I'm no longer afraid of you."

He laughed outright, steadying her when she wobbled. "Good. Since this is Friday, I expect you to drive home slowly and creep to work on Monday. Just make sure you're on time. Now let's get to work before you fall asleep."

"No problem." She blinked, yawning broadly. "I'm wide awake."

"Right. Then you certainly won't mind if I open all the windows to keep *me* from falling asleep?"

He did so, and cold air streamed into the room. She shivered, but he kept the windows open.

"Did you read the chapters?" he asked as they sat back down at the table.

She blushed. What would he say if he knew she'd been lying on the bed with Sarah while she'd studied? "Every word," she answered.

"And?"

"Very informative. The whole thing's a giant puzzle with most of the pieces out."

"Don't worry about it," Zack assured her. "Most of us had an opportunity to learn slowly. You're trying to rush. Show me how much you retained and we'll see where the holes are. Later I'll have one of our cameramen explain the rudiments to you."

The brisk air revived her. Zack's sharp questioning kept her mind searching for answers, and she was glad she'd reviewed the chapters after studying.

Often she'd bite her lip in concentration, only to look up and find him warmly watching her, his eyes thoughtful. He went over each page in excruciating detail, often praising her.

At last he leaned back, closing the book. "School's over. Monday, we'll go over this again, and the next two chapters too."

"What happens here on the weekends?" she asked, noticing the way he smiled, the whiteness of his teeth contrasting with his naturally dark skin. Two chapters weren't much, not if she got a good night's sleep and Sarah cooperated.

"Other than the cable caster sending satellite shows to our customers, nothing much. The place is deserted."

"I don't believe I recall seeing the cable caster."

He tucked a lock of her hair behind her ear. The casual touch sent flames racing down her spine. "Do you know what a cable caster is?"

"I haven't the faintest idea," she admitted.

He threw back his head, laughing. She realized with a start that his hand was now resting on top of hers and was stroking her skin. "A cable caster sends the satellite programs out to our customers. His office is on the other side of the building. Next time ask. It's the only way you'll learn."

Fully relaxed, she promised, then became instantly alert when he added, "By the way, I plan on taking you with me in the evenings when I'm directing. There's a basketball game at Rutgers Monday and I'd like you to come. Do you have a problem with that?" he asked.

His question, a direct challenge to Morris's edict that she leave at six, hung in the air.

She struggled with her response. He stared into her eyes, smiling enigmatically. "You'll never learn otherwise," he added.

It was true. Furthermore, Zack was giving her valuable assistance. Of course, the faster she learned, the less of a burden she'd be to him. And the less chance he'd have of asking personal questions.

An idea began to crystallize in her brain. Without thought, she sent him a captivating smile. "As long as you give me a few days' notice to arrange my schedule, which in this case you have, it's okay. I'd love to go with you Monday night."

Zack left her with David Kasdin, instructing him to show her how the Sony television camera worked. When he was finished with that, he was to do the same for the equipment in the control booth.

Leaving them, Zack headed for Morris's office. "Why is her resumé blank for last year?" he asked without preliminaries.

Morris looked up, his grizzled eyebrows raised. "Sit down, Zack. I presume you mean Hannah's resumé?"

Zack nodded as he sat. "This morning clinched it. Hannah isn't some yo-yo kid with a nursery-school attention span. I purposely overloaded her assignment. She handled it well." He stopped himself from adding, Even dead on her feet from an obvious lack of sleep, she's a darn sight brighter than most. She's eager. She's beautiful. And, dammit, she's desirable. She's also an enigma.

"I'm glad to hear you're impressed," Morris said. "However, I'm not her keeper, nor is this the CIA. We don't hire people for their personal lives, do we? Did I run a check on your private life?"

Zack never spoke about his failed marriage. He kept that part of his past under lock and key. "What's that got to do with it? You knew my ability. I had a track record."

"Precisely. And in a few weeks I expect you to know what she can do and put her where she'll do the most good for us." He leaned forward, brows knit. "The only important thing for you or anyone to know is that Hannah's ready and willing to do any task given her. You heard Madge. You said yourself she's bright."

"She is."

Morris was silent for a minute as he studied Zack. At last he said, "If you want to know about her background, ask her. But," he added as Zack started to rise, "I'd appreciate it if you give her time."

The pink pacifier loomed in Zack's mind. "Okay. But will you tell me why she needs advance notice to go on location in the evening? Who else does she work for?"

Morris steepled his fingers, looked him straight in the eye, and, because it suited his purposes, lied. "It's perfectly natural for a pretty, eligible woman to date on Saturday nights. Don't you date on Saturday nights?"

"Spare me the lecture," Zack snapped. He hadn't mentioned a Saturday night to Hannah or to Morris. All he'd said was that he planned to take her on location Monday night.

"All right," Morris said. "No lecture. I can only reiterate what I said before. Ask Hannah whatever it is you barged in here to ask me." His tone was noncommittal, smooth as the fifty-dollar silk tie he wore. Zack didn't trust him for a minute.

• • •

During lunch Hannah locked herself in one of the small bathrooms and pumped her breasts. She put the bottles inside the zippered lunch box she'd brought with her, then set the box in the employees' refrigerator. Half her lunch hour was almost up, and she dashed into an empty office to dial home. Phyllis assured her all was well. Hannah felt a pang of regret, then shook the silly feeling away. She must be some kind of nut, being jealous when her baby was perfectly happy without her. On her way out of the room, she bumped into Zack.

"How's it going?" He noted the faint purplish smudges of fatigue beneath her eyes. She was losing her second wind.

"If you need someone to photograph noses I'm your woman," she grumbled. "It's a lot harder than it looks. Your cameraman David is very good."

Zack smiled. She reminded him of himself when he first started. She was trying to learn everything at once. "You're right. He doesn't jerk the camera. Have you had lunch yet?" When she shook her head, he took her elbow. "C'mon. I know a perfect restaurant."

The "restaurant" consisted of two outdoor concrete tables and benches in a secluded picnic area not far from the employee kitchen. In the summer two huge oak trees would shade the latticed enclosure. No one else braved the blustery March winds to join them. Although there was a brilliant sun, Hannah wished it were ten degrees warmer.

"Breathe deeply," Zack said cheerfully. She shielded her eyes from the glare, squinting at him. "The brisk air will keep you awake."

They unwrapped their sandwiches, and Hannah wrinkled her nose at her cup of milk.

"Why drink it if you can't stand it?" he asked.

"Calcium is good for you," she said, changing the grimace to a smile as she quickly drank half of it.

"All the time?" he asked nonchalantly, his suspicions raised again. "Hannah, is there something else I need to know? To help you, that is."

She studied him for a long moment. It would be wonderful to unburden herself, especially since he'd been so patient, but she wasn't ready to take a chance.

She pulled her coat collar tighter around her neck and pretended to misunderstand him. "Yes, there is something you should know. Tomorrow I'll have coffee. If I need calcium, I'll take a pill."

His mouth tightened with annoyance at her evasion, and she quickly changed the subject.

"What did Madge mean by the ACE Award?"

A blue jay swooped down to peck at a worm in the ground. They watched his tug-of-war for a moment. "It's the industry's way of honoring its own," Zack answered. "The movies have an Oscar. Cable has this."

"And you've entered?"

He nodded. "Yes."

The breeze lifted her hair. He leaned forward, tucking it back from her face. She pretended not to notice, yet the simple gesture affected her more than she cared to admit. Not yet, she thought. She wasn't ready to feel yet. Controlling her wayward thoughts, she asked, "What happens if you win?"

"Presumably offers will come my way. I'll probably

move on, start my own production company. There are many things I'd like to accomplish. It's what I want."

She heard desire creep into his voice, saw it in his eyes. She remembered the day her ex-husband Larry had arrived home with two bottles of champagne and the biggest smile she'd ever seen spread over his face. He'd landed a new television job and, he'd told her, he was on his way to stardom. Excited, he'd whirled her around until she was dizzy. They'd celebrated. She was certain that was the night Sarah was conceived. But when Larry learned of her pregnancy, there was no champagne, no dancing for joy.

"Winning is very important to you, isn't it, Zack?"

"Winning is a long shot. Trying is very important. In golf there's a saying: Never up, never in."

"You don't like it here?" she asked curiously.

He crossed his legs, resting a hand on his knee. He didn't miss the interest in her voice, or the relaxed way she sat. "It has nothing to do with like. A station needs people who accept policies set down by management. Morris is a great guy. We just have different opinions on the future of cable programming. I'd rent time and stay here if I thought Morris would air all my programs."

"But isn't that a lot of extra work, added to your directing chores?"

"Sure, but anything worthwhile is worth going after. The thing is, Morris is definite in how he sees the future. Going out on my own would solve my problems. I can't fault Morris. He's making money, and that's the name of the game. I guess I want to do it my way."

"What would you do differently?" she asked, her sandwich forgotten for the moment.

He leaned his elbows on the table. "I'd offer more controversial programs, ones that aren't afraid to make a statement. I entered a different kind of story— *The Making of a State Trooper.* I'm proud of it, but it isn't controversial.

"Morris approves of this type of entry. He doesn't want to get into the other kind. If we air it from a national feed, that's one thing. No one can blame the station. I believe because of its freedom it's cable's strength, its obligation, to take creative leaps. Unfortunately, programming isn't up to me."

"I see," she said quietly. This was a man whose ambition would take him to the top. "And as you say, winning the award can help you achieve your goal."

He brushed crumbs from his pant leg. "You bet. The world loves a winner. Maybe my shows aren't as intellectually stimulating as I'd like, but I'm proud of them. By the way, Morris and I have discussed this many times. We have an honest exchange of ideas . . . except he always wins."

The sun dipped behind a cloud. Gusts of wind shunted across the ground, whirling pebbles, whipping up dust. Shivering, Hannah rose. Her eyes filled with pain. She knew about dreams and she agreed with him. He should leave if it would make him happy. "I'm sorry."

He stood and took her elbow. She held herself erect. "Don't be. I'm not complaining, just stating a fact. My time will come," he said with absolute assurance.

"Nevertheless, I'm still sorry."

He looked at her questioningly. "For what?"

"For not attaining your dream when you work so hard. I can see how unfair it must seem to you to be saddled with me along with all your other duties."

"Hannah, I wasn't talking about you."

She squared her shoulders and lifted her chin, and in her eyes Zack saw a flash of defiance. "Zack, we both know why you feel you're supposed to give me extra consideration. Please don't. I'm grateful for the opportunity to be here. That's enough for me. I promise to learn as quickly as I can. In fact, I have a few ideas on how to speed up the process. You won't be stuck with your shadow long."

"That's not fair. You're twisting my meaning."

She tossed her head. "Life's not fair, Mr. Matthews. My trouble was that I was dumb enough to forget it for a few minutes."

She walked away, her heels clicking on the pavement. She wasn't content to be only a homemaker, as appealing as that might sometimes be. But she couldn't think of that. She wanted a lot more for her daughter than the meager financial rewards of typing term papers, sewing, or arranging flower baskets at home.

Three

Zack sat back down on the bench and let out an exasperated sigh. He'd handled Hannah all wrong. Telling her about his professional opinions and differences with Morris was stupid. She'd misinterpreted his meaning. Sure, it was better for her to hear about it from him than from office gossip. Still, any fool could have seen she was tired and upset about getting a speeding ticket.

So what had he done to make her first day easier? Big, bad, intelligent director. He had teased her, grilled her like some kind of top sergeant who wouldn't let his rookie move until she came up with the right answer, and then he'd frozen her by making her eat outside. Yes, sir! He should be very proud of himself.

Morris had asked him to give her time. He should have picked up on the cues. He'd given her time, all right. About an hour. He wasn't long on diplomacy, not like Hannah. Now she thought he resented her. She'd likened herself to being an unwanted shadow. Nothing could have been further from the truth.

The best thing he could do now would be to leave her alone and let her enjoy her weekend. Monday he'd act as if nothing had happened. If she wanted to talk, fine. If not, they'd begin again when she was calm and refreshed. And this time he wouldn't poke his nose into her business. He wouldn't offer her coffee or decaf or milk. He wouldn't ask her about the pacifier, although he was curious as hell about that. Did she really baby-sit?

He watched a squirrel in one of the oak trees hop from bare branch to bare branch. In a way, the animal's restless movements reminded him of his life. He'd done his share of hopping around from branch to branch before he'd married. The wedding had been held in a country club, a lavish affair with her side of the family outshining his in number and panache, but not in warmth.

Lois had entered law school that fall with a burning desire to make partner in a prestigious law firm by the age of thirty-five. If long hours counted for anything, she should have made it by twenty-five. Once she was out of school and had a job, he rarely saw her.

"Don't you know by now they consider nine to five to be part time?" she said in answer to one of his repeated questions about her long hours at the office. "I want it all, Zack. And so do you. You're not home either, so don't take it all out on me."

"That's a lie and you know it!" he barked. But the fact was, she was right. They didn't argue, they just drifted apart. Sex became a ritual rather than a joy. One day, after they'd been married for more than four years, he came down with a bad flu. "Zack," she said, "I have an important case coming up. You don't want me to get sick, do you? Take the spare bedroom, just until you feel well."

They resumed an intermittent sex life, but it lacked commitment. The second bedroom became his as they chased their separate dreams. Gradually the chasm in their marriage widened. One night Zack waited up for Lois until she came home at two in the morning. His wife's eyes were unnaturally bright, her step cautious. Her hands shook as she laid her briefcase down on the table. "No case lasts this late," he said. He felt sick to his stomach.

She admitted there was another man in her life. A lawyer. It didn't mean anything. She had just gotten caught up. She needed time. They needed time. "A trial separation, Zack. It'll only be for a little while, for us to think."

Listening to her shrill tones, he had tasted bitter defeat. She was all sharp edges and angles, no softness. Her fling was no better than their marriage. Neither meant a thing to her. He threw himself into his work with renewed vigor.

Her firm handled the uncontested divorce. There was nothing to contest. No children. No valuable mementos. No community property either cared enough about to argue over.

He'd grieved, and wondered if she did too. For months tears would well up in his eyes at odd times. Marriage wasn't supposed to be like that, a tearing apart at the seams until the fabric frayed. Marriage was supposed to strengthen, to forge two people into one.

It was a terrible admission for him that he had failed in his private life. The past burned behind his eyes. For several years he'd told himself the best thing he could do was avoid another failure. That meant sticking to his resolve not to get involved with a woman again. His future was clear. All it took to get where he wanted was more hard work, more persistence, and a fair amount of luck when the judges voted. He didn't mind pouring his heart and soul into his entry for the ACE Awards. Either way he was going to make a break, and soon.

Hannah nuzzled Sarah's belly button. The naked baby lay on her bathinette, gurgling and happily waving her chubby arms and legs. Blue-green eyes gazed warmly into blue-green eyes. Hannah loved the tantalizing baby smells. "Mmmmm, your toes taste delicious." Sarah cooed, delighting her beaming mother. "So does your tummy and your tushy." The baby's eyes widened expressively. "The most scrumptiously scrumptious are these nice, juicy legs." Hannah sucked on the plump thighs, then carefully wiped them.

She kissed and dressed Sarah, then put her into her yellow sleeping blanket. "Into bed, pumpkin. You smell like a can of baby powder, my darling. Be a good girl. Mommy's got to burn the midnight oil studying."

It was almost noon on Sunday before Hannah set her plan in motion. Whatever she could do to speed the process along and not be Zack's shadow was worth it. Feeling good about her decision, she strapped Sarah into her car seat and drove to the studio. She located an unlocked door and walked down the long hall into the wing of the cable station that housed the control room Zack used. She set down the baby, reviewing what she'd learned from David about the monitors, the tape racks, and how to set the various equipment for recording. She flipped a switch, lighting the set. She did the same for the mike, making sure it was linked to the camera that was aimed at the chair she intended to sit in.

She quickly shed her coat, removed Sarah's outer bunting, and carried the baby onto the set. "Sarah honey, someday I'll tell you how Mommy started. Barbara Walters, you have nothing to fear."

Making certain her mike was attached to her collar, she sat in the chair Madge used to interview guests. Sarah cooed contentedly on her lap. For the next few minutes she tried out various introductions to imaginary guests, carrying on both parts of the interview, learning not to be nervous when she spoke. Sarah gurgled.

"Why thank you, Miss Sarah. Your answer was perfect. Here's your pacifier. Now for the sixty-four thousand dollar question. What do you think of the director, Zachary Matthews?" Hannah looked directly into the camera, then smiled at the baby.

Zack paused at the door to the editing suite. He could have sworn he'd turned off the lights in the control room when he'd left last night.

"And do you think he's handsome, Miss Sarah?"

Sarah kicked her legs. Hannah laughed. "Nice of you to speak so clearly."

Zack's ears picked up a familiar sound, and he walked quietly to the control room. He was stunned by the scene below. The mikes were on, the tape was running, and bright lights flooded the set. Hannah held a cooing baby in her arms.

"Oh, you think he's handsome," Hannah was saying. "I do too, except he frowns a lot. Now what would he say if he saw you, little pumpkin?" The baby began to fuss and cry. Her cries became louder, her mouth rooting against Hannah's breast.

Zack held his breath. He slid into his chair, his gaze fixed on the monitors and the scene below. Hannah kissed the downy top of the baby's head, shushing her with gentle, comforting sounds, then opened her blouse. His blood raced through his veins as she exposed a creamy breast. Shock and realization filled him at the same time. Hannah was a mother! The love in her eyes was overwhelming. His attention was riveted to her and to the beautiful baby in her arms.

"Shhh, Sarah," he heard her say. "I know you're hungry, my darling, and Mommy foolishly forgot to bring a bottle. We're lucky we're alone." She kissed the baby again as Sarah took the nipple and began to suck greedily.

Zack broke out in a sweat. This explained the pacifier, why she had to be home early, why Morris hedged in his answers, why she'd come in to work looking so tired. It didn't explain who the baby's father was or why she neglected to mention her family.

Stunned, he felt like a voyeur, yet Hannah and Sarah were so beautiful, he gave himself a moment. The baby was a replica of her mother, with curly brown-gold hair and eyes the same extraordinary shade. Her little pink cheeks sucked contentedly while her dimpled hands rested on the creamy globe of Hannah's breast. As the baby nursed, Hannah spoke lovingly to her.

Very quietly, he rose and left the room, giving her the privacy she deserved. He'd told her the studio was empty on weekends. She'd told him she wouldn't be his shadow for long. She certainly hadn't wasted time. He tasted the bitter knowledge of what she must think of him. She hadn't trusted him to tell him about the baby.

He waited by her car for her to come out of the building. He cooled his heels for an hour, an hour in which he thought of all the ways he'd tell her she should have had faith in him.

Hannah emerged from the building. As she walked along, she gazed down at Sarah, telling the baby what a wonderful "guest" she had been. Then she looked up and saw Zack. He was leaning against her car, his foot propped on a tire. Dressed in jeans and a tan leather bomber jacket, he was more handsome than ever.

Everything in her went still as he raked his wind-whipped hair back and pushed away from the automobile. His long legs carried him toward her, his face emotionless. She shivered in her coat, and her arms automatically tightened around her precious burden.

He stopped in front of her. Her pulses pounded.

She felt a familiar knot in her stomach, like the car sickness she'd suffered as a child. Zack's midnight-dark gaze seemed to penetrate her soul. Sarah's cooing sounded like a drumroll as he stared at the baby, then back at her.

The speech Zack had practiced in his mind died on his lips. He didn't want Hannah looking at him as if he were her enemy. Whatever reasons she'd had to keep her child a secret would have to wait. They no longer mattered. He didn't want to fight with her. He wanted to be her friend.

He jammed his hands deep in his jacket pockets. "She's beautiful. She looks like you."

"You were inside?" she asked tightly.

"Yes." He didn't want lies between them. For reasons he couldn't fathom, it was important there be no lies between them.

"Oh. I thought you said no one comes in there on weekends." Her voice was defensive.

"No one but me. I never dreamed you'd want to be here on your own. You should have told me about your baby."

The breath whooshed out of her. Seeing Zack had been a shock, but she realized what he said was true. She should have told him, and she was relieved that he now knew. Whatever was going to happen would happen. Sarah was hers. He could make whatever he wanted out of it.

Suddenly his words replayed in her mind. She heard his compliment again, spoken in a gentle tone. He'd called her baby beautiful . . . like her. He thought she was beautiful too. A little thrill coursed through her.

"You're right about telling you," she said. "But there were reasons."

He gazed at her intently. "Do they matter anymore?"

They stood silent for endless seconds, he stroking the baby's dimpled hand, she watching him. "No," she said quietly.

He smiled, and their gazes locked. "How old is she?"

"Almost four months."

He trailed a finger along Sarah's cheek, enchanted by the baby's soft skin. She stared up at him with bright eyes. "Where's her pacifier?" he teased, remembering it on his shoe.

Hannah's lips curved in a smile. She shifted Sarah to her other hip. "In my purse."

The words he wasn't going to say blurted out. "When I told you about the Rutgers game, you were thinking about her, weren't you? Why didn't you tell me? Why were you keeping this wonderful part of yourself a secret?"

She shrugged. "I wanted to tell you. I was going to, but . . ."

Trust, he thought. Morris had said she needed time. Somewhere along the way, Hannah had lost her ability to trust. A kindred spirit, he recognized that in her.

"May I?" he asked, holding his arms out.

Hannah glanced at Sarah, then at him. There was nothing to be afraid of. Their fingers touched and held for a moment as the transfer was made without a whimper from Sarah. She wondered if Zack felt the same tingling.

He held Sarah for a few minutes, awed at the feel

of her soft, warm body. When Hannah opened the back door of her car, he stooped and gently set the baby in her seat. He made certain the seat was securely fastened, then straightened. He brushed against Hannah, and heat rushed through him.

He cleared his throat. "Are these things safe?"

"It's the best car seat money can buy. Everything— the plastic construction, the molded frame, the straps—has been tested under the worst possible driving scenarios, including accidents. I read up on all the different models in *Consumer Reports*." Why was she telling him all that? she wondered. What was the matter with her? All she'd had to say was "Yes" in answer to his question.

"That's smart," he said. "You can't be too careful. Is she a good baby?" He couldn't stop looking at Hannah's mouth, staring into her marvelous eyes. "Are you sure your car is safe? You had trouble starting it Friday. Don't you think it should be checked?"

Hannah unbuttoned her coat. The temperature must have risen ten degrees, she thought. Or was the heat due to being near Zack? "No. I was nervous. I flooded the engine."

He nodded.

"That's why I've been drinking milk," she added inanely. "I mean, not because of the car. I want to give her the best start in life I can."

It made perfect sense to him, the conversation they were having aloud, and the one they were having silently. "Who watches her when you work?"

The wind carried the clean scent of him, filling her nostrils. "My neighbor. She's wonderful. Her name is Phyllis Fischer. She has two grown children. A boy and a girl. She's very reliable. If I give her adequate notice she'll watch Sarah in the evenings so I can go on location with you."

"I'm glad I know. Before . . . well, I treated you unfairly."

Hannah struggled with herself. "No, no. I realize now it was foolish of me not to tell you about Sarah, but I had my reasons. Morris wanted me to. It was difficult not to, especially after Friday." She was handling it all wrong, she thought, not making sense. "You see, I have to succeed, for Sarah's sake." She stopped, embarrassed. "I'm babbling."

He cleared his throat. "Where is Sarah's father?"

She met his gaze squarely. "My husband died the day after she was born. He never saw her."

He gasped and wrapped his strong arms around her, drawing her to him. She struggled to keep the tears from flowing and found her hands inside his jacket, reaching for him too.

"He must have loved you very much," he said quietly.

She trembled. "Love me, love me," she mumbled incoherently. "Love me." Her voice broke, and with each incantation the protective wall around her heart began to crack. "He loved me all right. He loved both of us."

Zack heard the bitterness in her tone, felt her stiffen. "Hannah, what are you saying? What happened with your husband?"

Shaking, she jerked away. Her fist went to her mouth, stifling the sobs she tried to conceal. "Nothing. I've already said too much. I'm going home."

He wouldn't let her. "Don't. Please. Not like this. Talk to me."

Her eyes burned. She clenched her jaw to hold back the tears. "Why? It's not part of my life now."

He curled her back into his arms, refusing to give her up. "It's very much a part of your life," he said gently.

She fought him. Tears of anger and regret brimmed in her eyes and spilled over, coursing down her cheeks. Gulping, she said, "Please, let me go, Zack." His breath was warm, tender, alive. "It has nothing to do with you."

"That's where you're wrong," he murmured into her hair. Her pain was like a knife slicing through him. He absorbed it, and his gaze slid to the baby playing with her hands in the car seat. Sarah and her mother were beginning to be very much a part of his life. "It'll help if you talk," he said. "Don't try to fight the world alone. Tell me. Let me help."

His tenderness was her undoing, crumbling her defenses. A tide of words erupted from her mouth as she released her pent-up emotions; in gushes, in gulps, in rage . . . in catharsis.

"I met Larry when I was in college and fell instantly in love. Crazy in love. I'd always been the cautious one in my family, but with Larry . . ."

She pulled back from Zack and shrugged expressively. Again feeling her pain, he took her hands and held them tightly.

"We married when I was nineteen. He was already making a name for himself in television, and he was determined to become big. I had no life of my own. He expected me to wholeheartedly support him . . .

live through him and for him. And I did. It's what I thought wives should do. I learned my lesson, because for Larry that wasn't enough. Whatever I did would never be enough."

She stared at her feet and her voice dropped to a hoarse whisper. "He had an affair with the wife of a big television producer and got an important spot on a new show. She did more for his career than I ever could."

She looked up again. "A few months later I found out I was pregnant. I was thrilled and excited. Larry . . . Larry wasn't. He left. I didn't hear from him at all throughout the pregnancy, and finally started divorce proceedings. Then, the day after Sarah was born . . ."

She remembered in vivid detail that horrible evening. She'd been lying in her hospital bed watching the news, waiting for Sarah to be brought to her, when the newscaster mentioned Larry's name. Her husband had been killed in a fiery crash when his red Porsche had gone out of control, diving over a cliff.

The doctor had found her on the bed, her head buried in her pillow, sobbing hysterically. The shock soured her milk for days. Finally, she'd seen that her widowhood was Larry's final legacy. His gift was a scary freedom—and Sarah.

"I took back my maiden name," she told Zack, "and I opened a bank account for Sarah's college education with the pittance left from Larry's estate. A couple of months ago Morris started talking about my moving here to Jersey and working for WBC. . . ."

Her voice trailed off as her anger began, once more, growing within her.

"I can understand his not wanting me, but Sarah . . . How could he not want her? He wanted . . . he wanted me to . . ." Her shoulders shook.

Understanding what she couldn't bring herself to say, Zack crushed her against him as if his arms, his body could wipe out the past, assuage the anguish. His hands found their way inside her coat, stroking up and down her trembling back. His lips brushed her forehead.

Drained, Hannah gradually quieted, then heaved a great sigh. She dug into her pocket, found a tissue, and blew her nose. She felt awkward. "I'm sorry. I shouldn't have done that. You caught me in a weak moment. I'm fine now. I don't usually make a spectacle of myself."

He tilted her chin up and wiped away the tears on her cheeks. "Hannah, you couldn't make a spectacle of yourself if you tried. I didn't know your husband, but any man who denies his child is no damn good in my book."

She sniffled, then smiled tremulously. "You sound prejudiced."

"I probably am," he said, grateful to see her becoming more like herself. "Don't forget, I held Sarah. She can make anyone a convert."

Hannah's heart pounded. Thoughts and emotions crashed around in her head, and she felt as if a great weight had been lifted from her shoulders. "Why is it that the last two times I've seen you, I've looked like a mess and sounded worse?"

He laughed. From the car seat they heard Sarah

gurgling happy baby sounds. They looked at her, and smiled. Neither one seemed willing to move, to break the contact.

"So," Zack said finally, "what do you say I follow you home and make sure there's no policeman on your tail? If you want we can go over some things you need to know."

Hannah was truly touched. "You don't have to. It's your day off too."

He squeezed her hand. "I want to. Okay?"

She brightened. She knew he was trying to make her feel better, to erase the scene from her mind, so she could come to work the next day without this hanging between them. "You're sure?"

"I'm sure. It's too nice a day to stay cooped up in the studio anyway."

He was right. The sky was a robin's-egg blue, the sun strong, the air warm. "Okay. Provided you let me fix lunch."

"Terrific."

"What's your favorite food?"

"Chili, the hotter the better."

"Will you settle for ham and cheese?"

"That's my second favorite," he said promptly.

She laughed. "Liar." It was good to talk freely, not to watch her words, to know she'd been wrong about him. "Zack, I misjudged you."

He grinned. "You're right. That's not saying I didn't give you cause. Let's go. Your daughter's fussing again."

As he pulled up for a red light behind her car, Zack smiled as he thought about Hannah. He didn't have to follow her home. He'd conned the invitation to lunch. Her car was perfectly fine. He had hours of work to do. All he knew was that he wanted to be with her. He wanted to see how she lived, to hear whatever she'd tell him about herself. He wanted to see her with Sarah, to hear her speak to the baby the way she had when she'd thought no one was in the studio.

Her home was situated on a cul-de-sac in a quiet residential community set on a hill. Dogwood, oak, maple, and pine trees surrounded the house. He parked his car in the driveway and followed her up the neatly trimmed stone path.

"Interesting collection of furniture," he said, admiring the well-ordered living room/dining room area.

Hannah laughed as she took off Sarah's outer clothing. "I call it early scavenger. If I were rich, I'd call it eclectic and would pay an interior decorator a fortune. There isn't a new piece of anything in the house, other than the couch. Everything else is either Salvation Army, garage sale, or things I've picked up here and there. All the slipcovers are new. I made them myself. As to the rest, you'd be surprised what an antiquing kit or a can of paint can do. Come see Sarah's room."

She led him into the nursery, and he looked around while she undressed the baby. Her talents amazed him. There was no self-pity in her attitude, just matter-of-fact pride.

"Did you paint the room too?" he asked.

"Yes. The elderly lady who owns this house said I can do whatever I want as long as I didn't knock down walls. She's really very nice. Unfortunately, she isn't too well."

He examined the painted furniture, the chest of drawers with its neatly stenciled flowers. "Did you paint the crib too?"

"Naturally. Actually it's a youth bed. I can make it longer someday. Painting spindles isn't the easiest job, but I love the look of them. One day I'll attach a canopy to the frame. This room is going to be a little girl's dream. All white eyelet and frills, with lots of stuffed animals and lacy pillows."

He envisioned it the way she pictured it. "Is that what you had when you grew up?" His room had housed soccer, baseball, and basketball equipment, and lots of team banners. It had never been neat.

"No. Mother was very practical. Money was never our strong suit. The furniture was sturdy maple."

He tried to imagine Hannah as a little girl. "Where do your parents live?"

"They both died years ago. I have a sister who lives in Texas, outside of Dallas. She's a pilot. She stops in every time she's in this area. What about you?"

"What about me, what?" He leaned down to peer at the framed pictures on the dresser top. Hannah and Sarah. Sarah and Morris. Hannah and a woman he guessed was her sister.

"Sisters? Brothers? Wife?"

He picked up a baby brush with a mother-of-pearl handle. "One brother. He lives in Vermont. I was married." He put down the brush and picked up a silver rattle. "We've been divorced for several years."

"Oh, that explains it. Would you mind handing me that box of diapers? This one's empty."

He handed her the box. "Explains what?"

"The time everyone says you spend in the office. Your driving ambition."

"You think that's bad?" he asked, piqued.

"Absolutely not. I understand perfectly. I don't have time for a social life either." No lie there, she thought. And there was no man on the horizon either. That suited her fine.

"How do you know I don't?" he asked.

"I—I wasn't thinking," she sputtered. She'd already heard about the bets the women at WBC placed on his dating, and one of the women had told her Zack's nickname was "Heartthrob."

"Don't assume. Anyway, don't you miss dating?" he asked carefully.

She picked up the baby, giving Sarah a smacking kiss on her cheek. "Not at all. I have everything I need right here. I have my priorities straight. Thanks to Morris and you, I'll learn and be able to earn a decent salary. I wasn't kidding when I said I'm a quick study."

She handed him the baby. "Play with her while I make us some lunch. You're very good at holding her head up, by the way."

The baby drooled on him. "Hey, she leaks," he protested, nuzzling the baby's little nose. He held her up above his head. She gurgled and drooled some more.

Hannah popped back into the room. Her eyes twinkled mischievously. "Wrong end," she said. "You'd know if she leaked."

Chuckling, he gathered the baby close to him, then followed Hannah into the kitchen. He leaned against a counter and watched her as she fixed a pot of coffee. Dressed in blue jeans, a blue shirt, and white sneakers with red laces, she could pass for a teenager. But, he thought, his gaze focusing on her full hips and rounded breasts as she moved around the room, she was all woman.

She swung round, her eyes glowing. "The coffee's decaf, by the way. Are you sure ham and cheese with mustard is okay?"

He smiled with satisfaction. "Perfect." She couldn't know his response had nothing to do with the menu or the fact that she'd invited him to stay for lunch.

Hannah trusted him with her baby. She was ready to accept his friendship. He was ready to help her. The quicker she could learn at the studio, the faster he could get on with his own goal. As far as he was concerned that was a fair trade.

Four

Zack played with Sarah for nearly an hour, saying he'd wait for lunch until the baby had gone down for her nap. While Hannah changed her, he strolled through her neat. home, discovering more about her in each room he entered. Rosemary, thyme, and chives were lined up in ceramic pots on the kitchen windowsills.

"Fresh is always better," she said when she joined him. She stroked the petal on a double-ruffled purple geranium.

"Gorgeous, isn't it? My sister flew this Martha Washington plant all the way from California. I had them in my garden when I lived there. I guess she knew I missed them." He smiled, thinking she was a woman who took pleasure in the simple things of life.

She stood in front of the patio door, the sunlight streaming over her. He wanted to tell her that her hair was beautiful, that her skin was as delicate as a flower, and that he was more interested in her expressive lips and what they'd feel like under his than in her plants. She glowed with a voluptuousness that made him itch to silence her with his mouth and stroke his hands over all of her. Instead, he dutifully looked at a huge red flowering plant in a macramé holder.

"Fuchsia," she said. Her finger slid over a leaf, as if to tell the plant it was doing fine. "I made the macramé," she added, then answered yes when he asked if she was responsible for the pair of needle-point pillows on the sofa, the bowl of clove-scented oranges in the bathroom, and the brightly painted musical mobile of circus animals above Sarah's crib.

If he sold his house that day, the new owner could move right in. The place was remarkably devoid of his personality. There were no pictures on the walls, no plants, no nicks or scratches on the white walls, nothing. It was as sterile as it was the day he had moved in. Aside from his books, his computer, and his desk, his house gave the appearance of a temporary residence, a place where a man could hang his hat until he decided what he wanted to do with his life. Not at all like the loving home he'd grown up in with his nurturing parents. It occurred to him as he watched Hannah dash back into Sarah's nursery to wind her musical mobile that she and his mother shared a common nesting instinct. Rented though Hannah's home might be, she'd put down roots as if the idea not to was abhorrent.

He smiled in memory of all his folks had put up

with while he was a boy. He'd raced from one hobby to another, his naturally curious mind sponging up the new knowledge avidly.

His mother and father had encouraged his interests. Most of the time. His father had frowned on his replacing the silver candelabra on the dining table with an ant farm. His mother had prevailed. With a sense of adventure and a prayer that the busy insects' glass cage wouldn't break, she'd allowed the ant farm to hold center stage, removing it only for Thanksgiving dinner when all the relatives came. They'd dined with the ants so often, eventually no one paid attention to them. His interest in the ant colony had lasted for six months; then his family had sighed with relief when he donated it to his science teacher.

There were other short-lived hobbies. Despite having no musical talent, he'd formed a rock group when he was sixteen. With her usual good sense of humor, his mother had donned fuzzy yellow earmuffs that sprouted like two giant suns on either side of her head. She'd glide through the house, protecting her eardrums until his interest waned. At the time he'd thought nothing of it, simply accepting his mom's good cheer. Years later, when he'd won his first award for a documentary about latchkey kids, he'd thanked heaven for his mother. She would approve of Hannah, he thought. She had never said anything, but he knew she hadn't felt his wife had been the right woman for him.

Shaking his head to clear away his reverie, he watched Hannah make their lunch. Two loaves of homemade rye bread were cooling on a rack on the counter, their aroma filling the kitchen. Hannah cut a third loaf for their sandwiches. She garnished the plates with cherry tomatoes and cucumber slices. Zack drank beer; she had herbal tea with a sprig of mint.

"This is delicious," he said after his first bite. "But tell me, when do you find time for all your hobbies?"

Hannah set her half-eaten sandwich down. "You'd be surprised how much time you have when you're alone in the evenings," she said quietly.

"No, I wouldn't." He noted the brief cloud in her eyes and patted her hand.

Momentarily flustered by his intense gaze, she sipped her tea. "Listen, I didn't mean to sound sorry for myself. I consider myself very lucky." She smiled, then leaned forward as if to let him in on a deep dark secret. "I earn extra money typing resumés, theme papers, things like that. I sew most of my clothes and do a bit of alterations too."

"I imagine you'll stop all that now."

"Hardly," she said, the serious look in her eye letting him know she'd given careful thought to her financial circumstances. "I'm in a training program, remember? Suppose I fall flat on my face—not that I plan to, mind you—but just in case I do, I'll still have an income until I land something else."

He waited for a long moment, then asked, "This may be none of my business, but didn't your husband leave life-insurance money?"

She shook her head and explained about Larry's inability to resist expensive cars and high-tech toys, like VCR's and computers. In order to buy those things, he'd borrowed heavily against their life-insurance policy. When he died, she got virtually nothing.

Astonished at further proof of how rough her past few years had been—and at how far she had come—he tightened his hold on her hand. "You're not going to fail, Hannah." Not if he had anything to do with it, he added to himself. Her husband had been a fool to walk away from a wife and child who were worth so much more than money.

Although he'd never met Larry Rivers, Zack knew all about him. Within the family of television, rumors and stories flew from coast to coast daily. Many were discounted, stemming from interoffice rivalries. In Larry's case, he had rightfully earned his reputation as a user. Hannah and Sarah had been discarded because they were liabilities.

Zack stretched his long legs out in front of him. He had to find a way to assist Hannah without having her jut her chin out and throw her shoulders back in defiant independence. Living alone and working as hard as she did wasn't fair. He sympathized with her and the legion of women across the country heading up single-parent homes.

But Hannah was special. Very, very special. She deserved happiness. Not that she was any of his business outside of the office, but he couldn't seem to help himself. She made him catch his breath just sitting across the table from him. He doubted she had any idea the effect her sensual beauty had on him. He toyed with his beer, trying to figure out exactly why he'd decided to become her savior of sorts. Suddenly she glanced up at him and smiled.

A spurt of warmth flowed through his body. He set down the beer.

"Hannah, as one friend to another, don't you think you ought to consider dating? Not all men are like your ex."

She coughed, then grabbed her tea and gulped some down. "Why? My life is fine the way it is."

He held her gaze with his. "It's not good to be a recluse. The longer you wait, the harder it's going to be."

She sighed in exasperation. "Zack, I haven't had a serious relationship or dated a man in so long, I wouldn't know where to start."

Just keep looking like that, he thought, and you'll have no trouble. Never had her lips looked more enticing, her eyes so trusting. "Don't you think you ought to try?"

She rolled her eyes. It was the same thing her sister said every week. "Go out, for goodness' sake!" Alex would exclaim. "Your eyes are wide open now. Have a little fun for yourself. It won't kill you. You might even like it!" Invariably Hannah ended the call by putting the whole subject out of her mind. Like taking a flu shot or swallowing foul-tasting medicine.

Now Zack, with his tempting body and handsome face, sat calmly offering the identical advice. Suddenly she felt very unsure of herself. Apparently the whole world shared the opinion that she was taking refuge in her solitude. How wrong they all were. She'd simply decided never to be hurt by a man again. That meant avoiding pitfalls. She tossed her hair over her shoulder. "I'm not comfortable with the idea of dating."

Having been there, he saw through her defenses and sympathized. She was scared and rightfully cautious. "I can understand that," he said. "After my divorce I was lonely, but I didn't have a Sarah to come home to."

He looked as if he regretted not having children, and she found herself asking him about it.

"To be perfectly honest," he said, "I thought I wanted children when I was first married. But my wife didn't. She had her career; I had mine. My work means a lot to me. I guess you can say it's my family. So everything works out for the best."

His tone was gentle, yet so filled with doubt that Hannah wondered if he'd ever marry again, perhaps become a father. He certainly was wonderful with Sarah.

She sat back, facing seriously for the first time what it meant to be alone. The world, she knew, catered to pairs. In advertisements . . . in restaurants . . . in travel . . . in married women friends afraid of competition. Had she been hiding all these months? Zack was intelligent and well-meaning. Should she trust him?

"It does get a bit lonely," she admitted, opening the door on her inner emotions a crack.

Zack flashed an encouraging smile. "I'd be glad to help you over the first hurdle. We could go out to a movie and have a bite to eat."

His offer stopped her cold. It was one thing to talk about dating in the abstract with him, quite another for her to be seen with him and let the gang at the studio believe her to be another conquest. "I'd better not. I have everything I need. Sarah and I are just fine, thank you."

"Sarah's an infant," he argued. "You're a grown woman. You can't keep using your baby as an excuse. It's only natural that you should see people your own age. Have some fun. I don't imagine you've had much experience with men," he added, his voice as gentle as soothing rain.

He saw he'd taken her by surprise, turning the conversation to such a personal vein, but then she kept surprising him too. She had since he'd first met her and been so captivated by her shining hair, her eyes the color of spring, the way she carried herself, the husky, sensual sound of her voice. He would offer her friendship first.

Suspicion wrinkled her forehead. "Do you always feel so sorry for strays that you ask them out?"

"Of course not," he said, refusing to acknowledge his idea was lousy. Why didn't he just ask her for a date without this beating around the bush? The answer came as swiftly as a bolt of lightning. He couldn't take a chance on her turning him down. And she would. She'd run like a frightened deer. For plenty of reasons, the least of which was his reputation at the studio. He knew she would have heard stories already and believe they were based in fact.

Hannah looked out the window at the tranquil azure sky. Why couldn't life be as peaceful? "If I went out with you, people would automatically think we were sleeping together," she said, then blushed furiously.

He almost smiled. He wanted to shower her with bouquets of flowers. Lilacs, roses, daffodils, lilies of the valley, violets, everything he could buy.

"But think," he said, grasping at straws, ready to

use his unearned nickname. "If we went out to-gether and you didn't succumb to my so-called charms, it would get around. Men would know they couldn't take advantage of you. Let's face it. You can make this work to your benefit."

Hannah picked up her sandwich. She chewed slowly, mulling over not only what Zack said, but what he hadn't said. His notion of helping her was riddled with illogical holes. It assumed too much, including the fact that he would know any man who might ask her out.

She opened the door to her emotions a little wider. "Suppose I do decide to date. What makes you think you'd know the man?"

"Think of me as family. You could introduce us and I'd let you know my opinion."

"Like my father?"

He threw his head back, laughing. "Heaven forbid!"

She gave him a false smile. The afternoon had been simply wonderful until he'd started this con-versation. He was making her stop and question her attitudes, what she wanted, who she was. It all boiled down to how much she changed, if she did change, she realized. Prior to her marriage she'd dated very little. Her idea of fun didn't include hop-ping into bed with a pimply, hormone-driven adoles-cent. Once married, she'd happily become Larry's loving shadow, doing his bidding, picking up after him like an adoring puppy. Maybe Zack and Alexan-dra and Morris and Phyllis weren't wrong. Perhaps it was time, after all, to take a chance.

"I'll think about it," she said.

He smiled broadly. Relief swept through him. "Good."

"I said I'd think about it. I didn't say yes."

He tried another tack. "Hannah, do you believe in love at first sight?"

She picked up her empty plate and carried it to the sink. Her hands were shaking. Turning on the tap, she waited a moment before answering. His question could plunge her into misery if she let it. She'd given up everything for love. For what? "Not anymore."

He rose and came to stand next to her. He lifted a lock of her hair, seemingly fascinated by the separate strands as they fell back into place around her slim shoulder.

"Neither do I," he said, "and that's exactly my point. Why spend all your evenings in solitary splendor?" He didn't tell her that he spent his evenings working, that his nickname had started as one of Scott's jokes and just hung on. "One of these days you're bound to fall in love and remarry."

"Not me. There are plenty of women who choose to live without a man." Anger at his persistence rose within her. "Do I look like a charity case to you?"

"Of course not."

She slapped a rag into the dishpan with such force, sudsy water splattered on both of them. "Then why this magnanimous gesture? Why not simply advertise for a woman on one of your call-in shows? Or place an ad in the personal column?"

He looked genuinely affronted. "That's not fair, but it only proves my point. Neither one of us is interested in marriage. With us it's strictly platonic; no one gets hurt. Besides, I like Sarah and she likes me. You can't argue with a winning combination.

Don't they say that children and animals are inherently smart?"

She glared at him. "Maybe I'd rather graduate from Dating 101 with someone else. Someone like Scott, for instance. He likes me and I like him. He asked me to go to the movies with him. What are you laughing at, dammit? Scott's a wonderful person."

He touched her earlobe, then grinned at her, pouring on the charm. "Hannah, I can't see you with a man who wears an earring."

She laughed in spite of herself. "Aren't you afraid I might have designs on you, Mr. Matthews?"

"You're much too sensible. Just look around this house and how you've organized your life. You're a woman who makes goals and strives to achieve them. I respect that. You already know I'm leaving WBC, whether I win the ACE Award or not. It's just a question of time. If you look at this logically, you'll see I'm the best man for you." She stared at him, at his mobile mouth, this glittering eyes, his strong chin. "Tell me, Hannah, do you believe in lust?"

She swallowed hard. How could she think clearly? She didn't know where to look. So she stared straight ahead, smack at his broad chest with its smattering of dark hair, revealed by his open collar. Unfortunately, it didn't help to be able to smell his aftershave lotion or know he was awaiting a response. "A little lust," she said faintly.

He tilted her chin up, then dropped his hands to her shoulders, inexorably drawing her closer. "I never thought of lust being doled out in small doses. It's an interesting point. Why don't we test it? In fact, lust might be a good subject for a show. We can't let Donahue and Oprah get ahead of us."

How did he expect her to think when he stroked her back as if he were deep in thought and needed some place to put his hands? "You were saying . . . ?"

He slid his arms around her. "I believe in attraction between the sexes. Adults have needs too." To prove it, he scientifically caressed her cheek with his, letting his lips graze her forehead. The simple action set off a tingling sensation down to her toes. "How does my touching you make you feel?"

It was a long moment before she found her voice, and she was disgusted when it came out like a squeak. "Very nice. Is this necessary?"

"Very nice good, or very nice terrific?" he asked, ignoring her question. "You need to be aware of your feelings so that when you begin dating seriously, you'll have something to compare it with. That's where I come in. Use me."

"Very nice terrific," she blurted. "But that's only because I live a celibate life."

He drew back. His eyes were very bright. Mischief lurked within them. "You hurt me, Hannah. I don't live a celibate life and I thought it was nice terrific." His hands cupped her face, tilting it upward. "Do you believe a true friendship can exist between a man and a woman?"

She mustered all her will. "I—I never thought about it."

"Think about it." His fingers found their way into her hair, rhythmically massaging her scalp. "I've given the matter a good deal of attention today. For instance, I believe a man and a woman can be good friends, kiss and enjoy it, and then part richer for the experience. Incidentally, that's a lovely perfume you're wearing. What is it called?"

She cleared her throat. "Golden Opportunity. Let's get back to your theory. What do you believe friendship between the sexes is?"

"A state of bliss," he said, completing the statement with a lingering kiss to the side of her neck. He savored the moment, breathing in her scent.

It was awfully hard, she thought, to keep up a conversation when electricity was zinging through her and she couldn't remember whose turn it was to speak.

"Hannah," he murmured, "you're a very desirable woman."

Her eyes flew open, and he smiled. "Mmmmm. And beautiful too. In fact, I feel extremely friendly toward you now."

The texture of his skin, the male smell of him, intoxicated her. "I feel quite friendly to you too." And then she threw caution to the winds, listening in disbelief as she said, "I'd be extremely grateful if you'd hurry up and kiss me before I have to go to Sarah."

His brows shot up. "Hannah," he said mockingly. "You shock me."

"That is where all this is leading, isn't it? Me and you kissing? So I can ease into being with a man and not get starry-eyed?" Where had she gotten the nerve to be so forward? She certainly hadn't been born with it.

"Of course," he said agreeably. "Your wish is my command."

Adrenaline-charged, she pushed away so she could look him in the eye. "Let me tell you what I believe, Zachary Matthews. I might be young and no doubt you top me in experience, but I know a line when I hear one, especially one as convoluted as yours. You're scared stiff I might have designs on you like the rest of the women at work. Rest easy, Heartthrob. If there's one thing I absolutely demand of a man since my lousy marriage went down the tubes, it's total honesty. I'm not looking for a commitment, just honesty." She poked his chest for emphasis.

"Hannah." He sounded pained.

"Frankly, I'm curious, not about all the mumbo jumbo you've been spouting, but about me, my feelings, and what, if anything, I'm going to do about men in my future. I want you to kiss me. It's been almost a year since a man's touched me. I admit to a certain sense of adventure, and maybe, just maybe, I might be ready to date again. I may even decide to go out with you, since you offered. So if you want to I'm ready, but on my terms. This is an experiment. You call it friendship if that helps you. Me, I'm chalking it up to curiosity. When it's over we both walk away friends. So what do you say? Do we kiss or not? Do we have a bargain?" She thrust out her hand, ready to seal the contract.

Zack smiled crookedly, hugging her. Her full breasts strained against him. "Are you always this direct?"

She looped her arms around his neck, curling her fingers into his hair. "As for this moment. You do understand that tomorrow we go back to work with no hard feelings. This is nothing personal."

His lips twitched in a smile. "I hope I won't disappoint you. I'm getting the distinct impression that if I don't perform well, all of mankind will suffer in your estimation and you won't want to go out with any man. Therefore, I'll have to do my best."

"I certainly hope so," she said impishly, then wondered who or what had taken control of her mouth. Was this really her saying these outrageous things, or was there a prankish elf inside her directing her words? Zack didn't give her time to think about it, though. He pulled her hard against him, letting her feel how much he wanted her.

"Afterward," he said hoarsely, "you can tell me if I pass. Oh, and by the way, I suggest you make up a list."

"A list?" She was too busy suppressing a slew of freely released scandalous thoughts. Thoughts of her and Zack facing each other on a bed naked, exploring the textures of each other's skin. Thoughts of his lips where Sarah's had been, tugging on her breast. Her heart began beating rapidly.

He traced her bottom lip with his thumb. "You don't think dating is just about kissing, do you? We have to go places. Parks, picnics, movies, ball games. That sort of thing. If I'm going to launch you, we'll have to do this right. I expect your full cooperation. I'll write down four, you write down four."

"That's eight dates," she said. "Ridiculous. Maybe one."

He gave her what he hoped was a sincere look. "We have to make sure you build your confidence. Friends help friends, remember? You'd do the same for me." He pulled her closer. "Now stop talking and let me get to work."

"On second thought," she teased, "maybe I should wait and do this with someone else."

"Much too late," he growled, his hand cupping the back of her neck. He smiled as a sigh escaped her lips. "Actually, it was the homemade bread that did it," he explained. "I'm a sucker for homemade bread. My mother used to bake bread. You brought out the nostalgia in me." He lowered his lips to within an inch of hers, paused, then touched the corners of her mouth, very lightly, first one side, then the other.

He was driving her wild with anticipation, banishing her nervousness. "After all this, do you intend to kiss me the way you kiss your mother?"

He rubbed his mouth against hers, igniting tiny flares. "Not on your life." He rained kisses on her cheeks and her eyelids. She resisted the urge to clutch, to devour. His teasing was more arousing than anything she'd ever experienced.

"Mmmmm," she murmured, beginning to clutch in earnest. His body was hard and muscular.

He nibbled her neck. Sweet, sweet nectar. "Lunch was delicious. This is dessert. My treat." He kissed her lips. "So good."

"This can't be happening," she gasped, already drowning in sensation. "I should have started dating months ago." He growled again and gave her a little shake, pleasing her enormously.

"In the name of friendship," he reminded her.

"In the name of friendship," she said, raising on her tiptoes and forgetting everything she'd ever told herself about becoming involved with her boss. He looked wonderfully, compellingly handsome. Virile. Low in her belly, her muscles contracted. His eyes closed as he crushed her to him.

She was dizzy. She felt as if her body were melting. She filled her senses with him. All afternoon she'd wondered what it would be like to have him press his body against hers. When he'd played with Sarah, his hands stroking her bare skin, she'd imagined him touching her skin, stroking her. Caressing her. Readying her. Imagined it so strongly, she'd felt it deep inside her.

His mouth closed over her moist lips, and Zack realized he was starving. His tongue went searching, his mission urgent, drawing to him the intoxication he'd only sensed before. He had meant to kiss her once . . . just a taste, he'd promised himself. A taste of elegance and he'd be satisfied.

Passion erupted in Hannah as he invaded her mouth. Long denied, she melded her softness to his hard body, oblivious to everything but the sensations guiding her. She was consumed by heat, drugged by an inner maelstrom. She was playing with fire when all she'd wanted was to test herself, to see if she were alive.

His lips blazed a trail over her face, down her neck. Their mouths became as one, and each heard the heartbeat of the other, wild and quick. Hannah strained toward him, a prisoner of her long-repressed desires. She became unaware of her surroundings as her emotions careened and collided.

Zack knew what she was feeling. The sweet pressure of her against him robbed him of caution, changed the rules he'd set. With rising ardor, he ground his hips to hers, murmuring his pleasure.

Suddenly her brain clamored for caution. It rang a warning bell in her head. What was she doing! Stunned, she twisted her mouth from his. They separated, staring at each other in astonishment.

When he released her, his jet eyes searched hers

for an instant. Each had rejected the folly of falling in love again—for Hannah, with a man who trod the path of her late husband; for Zack, with a woman who needed the security of a husband and father for her child. Thoughts of pretend dates and casual friendship vanished.

Zack tenderly took her face in his hands, attempting to make light of the kiss. "Hannah, I think we just proved there's no such thing as a little lust." He cleared his throat.

She nodded, swallowing the lump in hers. "True, but we proved friends can kiss and it doesn't have to mean a thing."

Or everything, they both acknowledged silently.

From the nursery they heard Sarah whimper. He gently squeezed Hannah's arm, patting it with quick strokes, knowing that if he let his hand linger, the temptation would be too much. "She needs you."

Hannah let her gaze wander over his lean face. "Yes."

He was torn between wanting to be there when she returned and never wanting to see her again outside of the studio. He wanted to pick her up and carry her into her bedroom and lay her on the white spread among the pillows and shams and explore her body slowly, leisurely, with his lips and his mouth and his hands. He wanted to wake up in the morning and see her face first thing, even before he looked out at the day. She'd smile and he'd know there was sunshine. They'd laugh. She'd poke his ribs and order him to bring in the Sunday paper. They'd fight over who got the comics first. He'd thought of little else but her since he'd first met her, and it stunned him. His life, the way he'd chosen to live it, his goals for the future, didn't include marriage. Not for years. And that's what it would take to keep a woman like Hannah.

His gaze slid down to her full breasts, then swept up to catch her watching him. Her face was flushed, and he imagined his was too. Neither spoke for a moment, aware of the heightened magnetism flowing between them.

"I'll see you at the studio tomorrow," he said. "Don't come to the door."

"Wait," she said. "Take the loaves of bread with you. I want you to have them."

She quickly wrapped them in foil, then shoved them into his hands. Sarah began to cry. With a shy smile she left him, knowing that by the time she finished nursing Sarah, Zack would be gone. But the memory of his arms around her, his mouth capturing hers, the searing heat of his body, would stay with her forever.

There'd be no dates with Zack. He'd be too easy to fall in love with, and she wasn't about to bleed twice. The Heartthrob wasn't for her.

"Are you checking up on me?" Hannah joked halfheartedly.

"Now what gives you that idea? However, if Zack's around I'd love to meet him."

She *was* checking up on her!

Zack flopped into a chair and scowled up at Scott. "Murphy's Law. Everything went wrong today. And we've still got the Rutgers/Penn State basketball game tonight."

"Bad day?"

Zack threw up his hands. "Awful. Everything that could go wrong did. Have you seen Hannah?" She'd been avoiding him all day. Each time he'd seen her she'd been occupied in her training program with another employee. He closed his eyes, remembering her as she'd been the day before. Hannah, her eyes glowing, her tantalizing mouth moving beneath his, her breasts pressed against his chest, her fingers digging fiercely into his back. She'd gotten under his skin.

"Did someone call me?" Hannah paused in the doorway, a vision in a pale blue dress with a lace collar. His pulse quickened and the very air he breathed seemed fresher. He smiled with pleasure.

"Tell me, pretty lady, do you have a cure for a rotten day?"

"Don't feel sorry for this big lug, Hannah," Scott said. "If you do he'll tell you all his troubles."

Zack flipped a paper clip in his direction. "Weren't you on your way out?"

Scott's glance went from Zack to Hannah. "As a

matter of fact, yes. I'm going to do you a big favor. I'll take the game tonight. You see, I do have a heart." He winked broadly, then closed the door behind him. Scott couldn't work the basketball game between Rutgers and Penn State alone, and both he and Zack knew it.

Not wanting to be disturbed, Zack got up and locked the door. "I really had a lousy day and I'm not in the mood to see anyone else." He sat down at his desk.

"I doubt if you have anything to worry about," Hannah said. "Everyone's gone for the night."

Zack grinned. "Was what I said to Scott as obvious as it sounded?"

Hannah smiled shyly. Her heart thundered in her chest. "Very."

"Good. I need a large dose of sympathy." He reached out his hand. "Come over here and be sympathetic."

"Talking to a friend helps."

He cocked his head. "Ahh, yes." He had something more personal in mind. Like kissing and making it better. His gaze slid over her. She was slim and poised, a serene, regal presence at the close of a frenzied day. He knew without being told that she was embarrassed.

"Have a seat," he said, wanting to add, *on my lap*.

She smiled at him. His shirt collar was open, his jean-clad legs thrust out in front of him, his hair disheveled from his fingers running through it. Grumpy and tired, a weak grin on his face, he was a sight for sore eyes. "As the director says, 'Shoot.' "

His grin faded as he clicked off his list of woes. "To begin with, some jerk bashes in my fender in a parking lot. Naturally this sterling citizen doesn't leave a note. That'll take a week to fix. Morris called an emergency meeting which wasn't. I barely had time to write the lead-in for the news. And I'm worried about Madge. She missed all of her commercial cues. She ran off the set at the end of the show without saying anything to the guests. Do you have any idea what's wrong? Scott doesn't."

"No, but I see the difference. At lunch she seemed to be clearing her throat a lot, as if she were having trouble swallowing. I don't think it's a cold, either. Madge is usually very perky."

"Whatever it is I hope it's minor."

Hannah hoped so too. Zack looked so disgruntled, and she tried to cheer him up. "You poor man. Hasn't anything nice happened to you?"

"Yesterday," he said, holding her gaze. "Yesterday was nice. More than that, Hannah. Yesterday was the beginning of something very important."

"Please, Zack," she said, resolved to nip this kind of talk in the bud. "We decided we'd be friends."

He sat up abruptly, leaning toward her. "I want to be more than your friend, dammit. I want to be your lover. I want to hold you and kiss you and not stop. Do you know what I'm saying? You're not just some woman I happened to meet. You're a valuable person and, what's more, I don't think you realize it."

"Please," she whispered, her eyes brimming with tears, her voice filled with regret.

"No!" He wanted to go to her, take her in his arms and make her forget all of her pain, but he knew that would frighten her even more. He softened his voice. "Ask me anything else, but don't ask me not to tell you how I feel. I spent last night wishing you were in my arms. Shall I tell you how I want to touch you? Where I want to touch you? How I want to hear you say my name and beg not to stop? Hannah, people can know each other for years and not feel as I do right now. If I didn't think you feel the same way, I swear I wouldn't be saying this."

"This is doing neither of us any good. Change the subject." Her voice sounded tinny in her ears. The things he said were true. She did want to be with him. She did want to kiss him, to beg him not to stop, but she'd learned a hard lesson in life: Don't wish for things that might come true—heartache is sure to follow.

"Is there something I can do for you?" she asked thinking perhaps she might knead the tension from his shoulders or fetch him a cold drink.

His expression made her feel light-headed, for she was aware of the leap of desire in his eyes, the sexual connotations he'd given her request. She felt herself flush. He opened his arms.

"How about a hug, friend?"

Her mind told her not to go into his waiting arms, not to react to his boyish grin, not to want. She was so certain she'd be able to resist him, but when he wiggled his fingers, as if to assure her he wouldn't bite, she uttered a tiny sigh and glided to him on winged feet, wrapping her arms around his strong shoulders.

"A tiny hug for a valued friend," she murmured, brushing her cheek on his hair. He smelled of lemony soap.

With a silent groan he clasped her to him. They

remained like that for endless tender seconds. No words were necessary. She gave him solace. He kissed the soft skin below her chin, inhaling her fragrance.

He didn't mean to do anything more than that, but he couldn't resist moving his head from side to side between the valley of her breasts, his lips wetting the fabric of her dress. She gasped at the sensation of his mouth, the hardness of his legs surrounding hers, the thrill of his hands trailing up and down her thighs, erotically connecting all the nerve endings in her body. She felt her nipples harden beneath his seeking lips.

"We're destined to be more than friends, Hannah."

She swayed momentarily. "We can't," she whispered raggedly.

"Why not?"

She wrenched away. "I'm not ready for this."

"Will you ever be?" he asked, tightly grasping her wrists.

"I don't know."

He released her and rose, every muscle in his body tense as he towered over her. "Maybe this will change your mind." He yanked her to him, crushing her against him, leaving no doubt as to his arousal. His lips were hard, demanding, his tongue invading her mouth. He was like a hurricane, buffeting her with the force of his desire.

Mindless, she responded, her lips moving beneath his with a feverish yearning. She was playing a dangerous game, testing herself with a passionate man. With a moan, he dragged her hand down to cover the rigid bulge in his pants, holding her fingers there until her raging desires ruled her motions.

Groaning, he eagerly sought the buttons on her dress, freeing her breasts. He buried his face between them as his mouth found the exposed nipple. Sucking, tugging, moving against her, he punished her with his expertise. She moaned, writhing, lifting and pressing her engorged breast into his mouth.

Sanity suddenly flooded her fogged brain. "No!" she gasped, twisting out of his grasp. She shook to the marrow of her bones, shattered by the rapture he'd evoked.

Breathing hard, he stared into her eyes. "You've been lying, Hannah. You want me as much as I want you. It's about time you grew up."

Though passion still throbbed within her, she managed to hold his gaze. "You're right in one respect. I've acted improperly. I've lied to myself. I did want you. I even fooled myself into believing we could be just friends. I'm sorry for leading you on, but you're to blame too. I reserve the right to change my mind. We're just two employees who happen to be working for Morris Winger, and neither one of us better forget it."

He shook his head sadly. His glance fixed on the hand that had briefly caressed him, then swept up to her eyes.

"Have it your way, Hannah. It's too bad you don't realize that what's between us is more than sex."

Terrified to unlock her feelings, she looked away. "I can't discuss this."

She hurriedly fixed her clothing, then unlocked the door and flung it open. "Just a minute," he said. "You're going tonight to the game, as planned. It's time we speed up your learning process. We each have things to do."

"Fine," she said bravely. "I'll tell Scott I'm ready."

"Never mind that," he snapped. "Scott was teasing before. I'm directing. You're going to practice technical directing. When I say push a button and change cameras, do it. In fact, Hannah, you're going to do everything I say. If you don't like it, take it up with Morris."

She held back her tears until she was out of the room. What was the matter with her? Would she ever be free of doubts? Of placing obstacles in her way? Her actions were inexcusable. She knew she was more to blame than Zack. He made no bones about his wants. At least he was honest.

They piled into the van, affectionately dubbed Hippo. Its cramped quarters contained a complete remote-control room from which Zack directed his crew. The camera operators on the floor and in the bleachers, along with the game's commentators, viewed the game live. It was up to the director, using split-second timing, to know which camera to ask for. Zack had once called directing the art of instant and constant choreography.

True to his word, he kept Hannah hunched over the switcher board as he gave orders, showing his displeasure when she was a fraction of a second late with the call. Scott frowned, glancing from one to the other as he maintained the counter on the tape rack and set the tape for reruns.

"Listen, guys," he said at one point, "let's lighten up. I know you've had a bad day, Zack, but what the heck. This is only a game."

"Like hell," Zack retorted. "Everything I do I do to advance my career. Hannah knows that. I'm surprised you forgot."

Baffled, Scott turned to her. She ducked her head, biting down hard on her bottom lip to prevent herself from speaking.

After games, Zack and Scott usually stopped at a diner for a bite to eat and to talk over the calls. It was a method both used to unwind. When Scott asked where they should go that night, Zack tersely answered, "Too busy tonight, Scott."

Zack drove them back to the studio, removed the tapes, locked up the van, and strode inside. He never once told Hannah if she had done well on her first attempt.

"Hannah," Scott said, taking her arm. "This may be none of my business, but I've known Zack for years. Until you arrived he was a nice, easygoing maniac. The only person he drove was himself. I've never seen him this mad. Care to tell me what's going on between you two?"

"Absolutely nothing is going on." Her unflinching gaze dared him to contradict her. "Your friend"—she hated that word now—"is a baby, that's all. When he can't get what he wants, he throws a tantrum!" Giving every indication of wanting to throw one herself, she stalked off.

Thursday evening Hannah drove to Teterboro to pick up her sister, who'd flown a group of businessmen from Texas there on their corporate jet. The two sisters hugged each other in the lounge, then Alex stood back to give Hannah a long, critical appraisal.

"On the surface you're fine. I don't like what I see

underneath." She handed Hannah her overnight bag. "Let me do the necessary paperwork for the flight, then let's get some food. My treat. Aren't I generous?" She laughed, her green eyes sparkling.

They found a restaurant near the airport, ordered, and chatted about Sarah. Alex dug into her food with gusto. Hannah picked at her chicken salad. She'd lost her appetite since her fight with Zack. The last few days he'd treated her with polite coolness. She'd been assigned to work with Scott, perfecting her responses in technical directing. Hannah told Alex that, then added, "Madge is after me to try my hand at interviewing. I must not be very good behind the camera."

"Whoa. Back up. Number one, who's Madge and Scott? Number two, you implied *another* person said you should be in front of the camera."

"Sorry, sis. Scott and Zack are more or less a team. Madge hosts a talk show. Getting back to the men. Each directs or TD's. Technical directs or switches the camera by punching buttons when the director calls for a different shot."

"Why can't the director do that?"

"He can, but everything moves so fast. It's hard to keep track of setup shots and what the audience is seeing at the same time."

Alex waved her sandwich. "Never mind. Tell me more about Scott. You lost me on the rest."

"Scott's nice. Very Irish. Very laid-back. He sucks a different color lollipop every day, depending on the day of the week. It's nutty, but after a while you think it's normal. And he wears a diamond earring."

"He sounds like someone I might like. Is he married?" Hannah shook her head. Alex's eyes bright-ened with interest. "Ever been?"

"No. He's happily single. Like I am."

Alex hooted. "If that puss of yours is happy, spare me seeing it when you're unhappy. How come you've avoided talking about Zack? Last week he was topic number one."

"There's nothing to talk about," Hannah said, shut-ting the lid on the subject. "We had a misunder-standing and agreed to disagree. He wants more than I can give. That covers it."

Alex sipped her iced tea, a thoughtful look on her face. "If you're not going to finish that salad, let's take it with us. I'll have it later. By the way, I called Morris. He's invited me on a tour of the studio to-morrow and the three of us will have dinner tomor-row night. If you can't get Phyllis to take care of Sarah, bring her."

As it turned out, Phyllis was only too glad to watch Sarah.

Because they were going out to dinner directly from the studio, Hannah arrived for work in one of her prettiest dresses. Its turquoise color was the perfect complement to her eyes. A wide black belt showed off her narrow waist, and the softly draped bodice emphasized the gentle swell of her bosom.

Alex arrived at the end of the day. Hannah waited on the sidelines while Zack filled in for Morris, giv-ing Alex a tour of the studio. Dressed in a blue pin-striped suit, a white silk shirt, and dark blue tie, he was so attentive to Alex that Hannah in-wardly fumed. He was flirting with her sister! More-over, Alex was having the time of her life. Hannah was so intent on the two of them, she didn't notice Scott until he nudged her arm.

"Introduce me. Zack's monopolizing her time and I want a chance too. Where have you been hiding her?"

"I haven't." She stood as stiff as the walls, besieged by misery. Zack was living up to his nickname, charming Alex. And Alex was falling for it.

Hannah spun around, not wanting to see any more. Since when did her sister move in on her territory? With a dull ache, she realized Alex had a perfect right to do as she pleased. Hadn't she spent the better part of the previous night convincing Alex Zack meant nothing to her?

"Here you are," Alex said, walking up to them. She looked adorable in a black velvet toreador jacket over a long-sleeved white blouse and full red skirt. Zack stood by her side, the perfect host. Hannah introduced Scott to her sister, refusing to look at Zack.

"I'll go get Morris," she said, anxious to separate herself from him. Alex excused herself, catching up with Hannah.

"Zack's joining us tonight."

Hannah made no effort to hide her dismay. "You know how I feel about him. If you want to date him, that's your affair. I warn you, though, he's a fast worker." She stiffened, sick at the thought of Zack kissing Alex, of his making love to her. "I thought this was a family night."

Alex shook her head. "For goodness' sake, you're getting this all wrong. Morris asked him this morning, not me. Then he palmed me off on Zack. What was I supposed to do? Tell him I can't speak to him because you refuse to make love to him? How childish do you want me to be? The man was polite and informative, nothing more. Personally, I think he's crazy about you."

"The man is crazy. Period." Consumed with curiosity, Hannah asked, "What do you mean, he's crazy about me?"

"It's obvious, and if you weren't so blind you'd see it. He eats you up with his eyes when he thinks you're not looking. I'm beginning to think you're going to be alone the rest of your life. Keep up this attitude and I'll be sure of it."

Hannah crumpled. She really was losing it, just as Alex said. Yet she couldn't seem to take that quantum leap where trust replaced suspicion. "Do you really think so?" she asked.

Alex threw an arm around her. "Yes, you silly goose. I know so. Now go repair your gorgeous face. We're double-dating. You can choose either Morris or Zack. Who will it be?" she teased.

Hannah shook her head. She wasn't ready to choose. She'd let the chips fall where they may and see if her sister was right. They found Morris in his office, then walked back toward the control room.

"Ready?" Zack asked Alex, ignoring Hannah as he slipped Alex's coat over her shoulders.

Morris helped Hannah with her coat, then the four of them walked out to his Mercedes. "Nice night," he commented as they neared the car.

"Lovely," Hannah said. The stars were out and the wind had died down. She slipped into the front seat and adjusted the safety belt. "Where are we going?"

Morris craned his head around to the back. "Zack, you're up on all the in places. What do you suggest?"

"Morris, I was under the impression we were going to conduct a little business and then you'd have the rest of the evening with your nieces."

"So I'm combining both, so what? Where's a good place? Alex is new here. I want to show her a good time."

Zack shrugged. "How about Southern Jim's? Alex might enjoy it. The food's good and the bands start playing at seven." He turned to Alex. "Do you like to dance?"

"Love it," she said.

Hannah sagged, lost in the misery she'd created. Zack's about-face meant he wanted to be with Alex at the very place she'd picked for a date. Southern Jim's, fashioned after restaurants in the roaring twenties, featured seven dining rooms, each distinctively different in decor and ambience. Depending on one's preference, there was cabaret music, jazz combos, a disco club, and featured guest artists. It was a lively, popular place, and Zack had just spoiled it for her.

"Morris," she said, "that's a place where you dine and dance. I don't have that kind of time."

"Don't be a spoilsport, Hannah," Alex said. "Southern Jim's sounds fine."

Hannah wanted to kick her. "I've got the beginnings of a headache. Look, drop me off at home. The rest of you can go on."

"No," Alex said swiftly. "Phyllis said she'd stay with Sarah as late as you wanted her, remember? Southern Jim's sounds like fun. I'm the visiting guest. Humor me. I promise your headache will vanish as quickly as it came. You're probably hungry."

When they reached the restaurant, Morris decided

on the dining room featuring music from the forties and fifties. "When I dance, I want to hold more than air," he said. "How about you, Zack?" Zack grunted.

Hannah would have preferred some blasting rock and roll so she wouldn't have to think or engage in conversation. Zack courteously removed Alex's coat and handed it to the coat-check girl, then escorted her into the dining room, pulled out her chair, and sat down next to her. He'd chosen, and was letting Hannah know it. Morris, apparently oblivious to what was going on, waited while Hannah shrugged out of her coat and then checked it. As soon as she'd seated herself he began to ask her questions about the various listings on the menu, acting as if he'd never ordered anything for himself in his life. She knew very well Morris led an active social life, yet he was pretending to be a country bumpkin. Hannah was starting to seethe.

The waitress arrived to take their drink orders. Hannah started to ask for a mineral water, but Zack cut in. "She doesn't drink. She's nursing." Hannah gasped. Alex giggled. Morris took it in stride.

"I'll have a white-wine spritzer," Hannah said to the astonished waitress. Zack slapped his napkin on the table.

"Well," Morris said, his voice ebullient with fellowship and good cheer. "We're off to a wonderful start this evening." He peered from a scowling Zack to an infuriated Hannah. "I'm glad to see you two hitting it off so well. I like to think of us as one happy family. Zack, you should be hearing soon about the ACE semifinals. Hannah, has he told you about the documentary he's entered in the ACE Awards contest? You ought to get him to air a copy of it for you. It's very good. Say, this was a great idea you had, Alex, suggesting that Zack accompany us." Alex ducked behind her menu, avoiding Zack's and Hannah's startled glances.

The waitress arrived with the drinks. Hannah took a very unladylike gulp of hers, then fortified herself with another. She quickly downed the entire glass, giving herself permission to get through the evening. When she ordered beer-battered shrimp, she loftily raised her chin in Zack's direction.

"Hannah honey, I have a favor to ask of you," Morris said while they ate their appetizer of mushrooms stuffed with crab. "Actually, it was Madge's suggestion and I concur. She was supposed to attend the television/media expo with Zack next week. It runs from Wednesday through Friday at the Javits Convention Center in New York. She thinks it would be a great opportunity for you if you went in her place."

"That's wonderful!" Alex said. Zack shifted in his seat, watching Hannah.

"Whatever for?" Hannah asked, her mind racing to the personal problems sure to arise.

"Madge thinks you should attend the seminars on hosting talk shows," Morris said. "It's a fine idea, Hannah. While you're there you should attend a seminar on directing, too, so you'll get a better idea of what's involved. If you've never seen the center, it's quite an experience. It's located right on the Hudson. Zack could arrange it."

"But why would Madge suggest such a thing?" Hannah asked.

Morris sat forward, leaning his elbows on the table. "I know you've noticed the problems she's been having. It's medical. Madge gave me permission to tell you if I thought it necessary. She's going to be taking some time off."

"What's wrong with her?" Zack asked.

"She needs a thyroid operation. You've heard how husky her voice is lately. When she began to have trouble swallowing, she decided to check it out. She's had a CAT scan and seen several doctors. All agree there's a tumor which must be removed. They've scheduled the surgery in two weeks."

"Aren't there others more qualified to fill in?" Hannah asked, still in shock.

"Madge wants you. She's very astute. If she feels you are an asset, it doesn't matter to her that you're inexperienced. Between now and the time you'd start hosting the show, you'd be doing segments, getting some time on camera. And she wants to train you. She feels it will lessen her anxiety while she waits to check into the hospital. Zack'll coach you too."

"I—I don't know what to say," she stammered.

"You have to say yes," Alex urged, which didn't surprise Hannah. "If Madge thinks you'll do fine and Zack helps you, what's the problem?"

The problem, Hannah wanted to shout, was Zack, and Alex knew it. He'd maintained a stony silence. "Go," Alex said. "It's good business. Don't worry about Sarah. I'm dying to get to know my niece better. I'll stay with her. Phyllis can help me."

"What about the businessmen you flew up here? Don't they have to go back?"

"That's no problem," Alex said. "There are other

pilots who'll take them. I'll hop a ride home. It's done all the time. I told you I have vacation days coming. If I get bored, I'll call Scott. I understand he plays a mean game of backgammon."

Hannah resisted the urge to strangle her meddling sister. When did she get so interested in Scott? They'd barely talked. Her obvious ploy took the cake. Zack, no doubt, was annoyed too.

"Zack," Morris said, "you haven't said anything. Don't you agree it's a great idea for Hannah to guest-host Madge's show?"

Zack slid back in his chair and stood up. "Excuse us." He grabbed Hannah's hand, practically yanking her out of her chair. "Hannah and I need to talk. Let's dance."

He whirled her onto the dance floor, swinging one arm around her waist and enclosing her right hand in a tight grip. "All right. What the hell is going on?"

"I know as much as you do. I can't imagine why Madge thinks I'd be a good replacement for her." She scowled at him, her agitated thoughts demanding release. "Don't worry. I have no intention of going anywhere with you. I'm sick of this whole mess. You're safe. So why don't we go back to the table and stop this farce?" Despite her irritation, she was struck once again by his handsomeness, his masculinity. She quelled her traitorous thoughts.

"Not yet," he said.

"Why not?"

"If we go back to the table with Morris beaming and your sister playing Cupid, I'm liable to say something I'll regret." They danced in silence for a minute, tense, acutely aware of being so close to each other. Around them the music swirled romantically. Hannah's pulse began to throb.

"This can be an opportunity for you, Hannah," he finally said, offering his professional advice. "Madge isn't wrong."

She nodded. How long could she be in his arms and not surrender to her innermost desires? "I'm aware of that," she said, sounding unenthusiastic.

"Opportunities don't come often, Hannah. Don't let too many of them pass you by."

She understood his innuendo. She thought of Sarah and her future, weighing it against being with Zack for three days. She was trembling. His jet-black eyes watched and waited.

"All right," she said finally. "I won't let Morris and Madge down. I realize this is a golden opportunity. So I'll go. Now let's sit down."

"No."

"Why?" she managed to ask. She didn't know how much more she could take of his closeness. His thigh kept brushing intimately against hers. He moved like a sleek cat.

"Because I'm stupid enough to want to be miserable with you. Now be quiet and dance." If it were possible to hold her tighter, he'd just found a way.

Hannah melted at his backhanded compliment. She hadn't felt so happy in a long time. She snuggled up to him.

"Don't get any fancy ideas," he said, a slow smile spreading over his face. "I just needed a fix."

"Who's complaining?" She glanced up at him. She was sunk and she knew it. "I'm sorry about what happened."

They were practically standing still. His chin rested atop her head. "How sorry?" he growled.

"Very," she murmured.

"I should have gone slower," he admitted ruefully. "My good intentions fall by the wayside where you're concerned. We'll try it your way."

She sighed contentedly. "Thank you. It's a little hard for me, but I think I'm on the right track. I'm not as afraid as I was."

He gave her an affectionate squeeze. "You look beautiful." She traced his ear with the tip of her finger. "Stop that."

"Why, I thought you liked this," she said innocently.

He groaned. "I love it, but you're not going to be wearing clothes if you keep this up. Then what will your matchmaking sister think?"

She tilted her head to look up at him through her lashes. Morris and Alex danced by. Alex winked. Morris waved.

"Hannah, will you drive to the conference with me?" Zack asked. "Stay in the same hotel?"

A lifetime passed as he waited for her answer. Both knew what their being together would lead to. She knew he'd be leaving with the right job offer. As she gazed into his eyes the decision became inevitable. It was time she took the next step in life. A step she wanted to take only with Zack.

"Yes," she said, sealing her fate.

Six

Zack stepped into the control room. The set was lit. Hannah sat in the chair reserved for the talk-show hostess, Madge in the "talent" seat. He watched for a moment, listening to Hannah's smooth, even delivery. Dressed in a blue sweater and blue pleated skirt, she'd pulled her hair back from her face, making her blue-green eyes seem larger. He concentrated on her ripe, full mouth, imagining it under his, his tongue stroking her as she gave herself to him. He blinked away his heated thoughts. Still, he knew that regardless of the subject, once a man saw that face he wouldn't be switching the dial.

A current of emotions swept over him. The previous night, Monday, he'd brought Chinese food to her house. Alex and Scott had made it a foursome, then gone to a movie. Hannah had let him help bathe Sarah. When she was asleep they sat in the living room, practicing. He used a stopwatch to cue her for commercials, but had a hard time concentrating on what they were doing. After his divorce his parents had told him that one day he would find his true soul mate and fall in love. He'd scoffed at their platitudes, the homilies offered to assuage his grief. How could loving someone make you happy? Yet as he'd sat in Hannah's living room, engulfed in the flames of arousal she'd sparked in him when they'd first met, he'd wondered if this was what his parents had meant.

"What do you think, Scott?" he asked now. "How's she doing?" He wanted an unbiased opinion.

Scott eyed the monitors. "She's getting there. In fact, I think she's got the makings of a real talent. She has a naturalness that can't be faked. Unfortunately, Madge fires off instructions. She's covering too much at once. Hannah tries to keep up. Between the two of them I'd say the sooner her baptism by fire is over, the better for all concerned. It's a good thing she's going with you. The seminars will bolster her confidence. She's better than she realizes."

Zack patted Scott's shoulder. "I know, but you can't blame Madge. She went out on a limb selecting Hannah."

"Do you think she was wrong?" Scott asked.

"Heck, no. From the first Madge said Hannah's rightful place was on camera. Look at her. She's fresh. She's bright and she's beautiful. She'll have every man drooling, and the women will try to imitate her. She radiates sex and trust. I'd say that was one hell of a combination."

Scott unwrapped a green lollipop. "I'd say you were some kind of prejudiced."

Zack grinned. "You're right. I'm going down there. Hannah looks calm, but I know she's frazzled." And he knew she was worried about leaving Sarah.

"Hi," he said as he walked onto the set.

Hannah looked up. Meeting Zack's penetrating gaze, she felt warm and beautiful. Was he thinking about the steamy kiss they'd shared the night before? she wondered. And then the next, and the next, when neither had been able to say good night. She was falling in love. It was a scary, wonderful feeling.

Madge peered at him. "Hi yourself. We were just going over a few last things. Hannah's interviewed me. She went into the commercial without a hitch." She reached over to squeeze Hannah's hand. "She's going to do just fine."

"I agree," Zack said. "Now, ladies, I'm breaking this up. There's such a thing as overkill. Madge, go home and play with your husband. He's called twice and threatened to send out the militia."

"I'm going, I'm going," Madge said, then called back, "Break a leg, Hannah."

Hannah laughed and waved good-bye, hoping that some of Madge's ability and expertise had actually rubbed off on her.

The next morning, Zack arrived at Hannah's at eight A.M. to drive with her to the convention. Even after her suitcase and carryall bag were packed in the car, she kept finding reasons to go back into the house and kiss Sarah one last time. Finally, Alex couldn't stand it.

"Zack," she complained, "get her out of here. She's driving me nuts."

"But I really have to get one more thing," Hannah said, wedging her way between Zack and Alex, who were blocking the front door. Despite her list of reminders covering everything pertaining to Sarah, she'd nearly forgotten the two things she needed— her breast pump and her nursing pads, to hide any possible leaks.

Knowing she finally had run out of excuses, Hannah held Sarah one last time. Watching her, Zack figured he must be nuts too. *He* was experiencing pangs of regret at leaving the baby. She was holding her little hands out to him and smiling her most winning smile.

"Come on," he said gruffly to Hannah, and at last dragged her into the car.

"We're only going over the state line," he said as they drove away. "It's not even thirty-five miles. There are phones. If anything happens we'll be back in a jiffy." She looked so upset, he was sorry he'd planted a negative idea in her head.

"Nothing's going to happen," he added, taking hold of her hand. "Stop being a wreck. Between Phyllis and Alex, they've got things under control. How big is Sarah anyway? What can she do to two grown women?"

"I can't help it," Hannah said. "I've never been away from her for so long before." She bit her lip and leaned her head back on the seat. She knew she was acting foolish.

Zack squeezed her hand, glancing at her. He admired the proud tilt of her chin, her determination to succeed. With all that was about to happen to her, that would thrust her into the limelight, being a mother was Hannah's most treasured and important role. He knew what an effort it was for her to relax. Much later, when the day ended and they were alone, he'd show her how much she meant to him. He'd shower her with the growing love he felt for her.

"Sarah's in better shape than I am," she said.

"I wouldn't say that. Sarah's got a long way to go to be in your shape."

He abruptly pulled the car over to the shoulder. Setting the emergency brake, he turned to her. "Listen, Hannah, I know you're nervous, but Madge isn't expecting more of you than you're capable of delivering. Scott and I watched you in the booth yesterday. He thinks you're a natural, and so do I. Another thing: Morris would never put his show on the line if he didn't have faith in you."

Hannah nodded. It was time to bury the doubts Larry had instilled in her and prove her worth. "Don't forget," Zack added gently, "I'll be directing you."

She threw her arms around his neck. "Thank you. I needed that."

"Yes, you did. Honey, get your priorities straight. Sarah's fine. She didn't even cry when we left. It's your turn." He wanted to say it was their turn, but wisely kept silent.

As if they were on the same wavelength, Hannah wondered about the hotel arrangements. All he'd said yesterday was that they were taken care of. He'd told her to ease up, and he was right.

The rest of the trip to glittering New York City

passed quickly, and soon they were entering the Javits Convention Center. They joined the throngs of media and television people signing in. Several conventions were being held in the huge place at the same time, and the center hummed with activity.

"A lot of people come here to buy programs for their local stations," Zack explained. In addition to gaily decorated welcome booths, small areas were set aside for salespeople and purchasers to hammer out negotiations.

As they passed a Sony exhibit, Zack paused to ask a question about a new camera. Hannah excitedly tugged his arm. "Isn't that Dan Rather?" No sooner had Zack said yes than she tugged him again.

"Jane Pauley," she breathed. Her eyes shone with excitement.

Zack leaned down to whisper in her ear. "That's going to be you one of these days." He tweaked her nose.

"I can't stand it," she blurted. "I'm so excited. How do you stay so calm?"

"Who said I'm calm?" he asked, his warm gaze traveling over her body. "Wait until I show you how excited I can get." Hannah blushed to the tip of her toes. He had just left no doubts as to the sleeping arrangements.

Zack told her the convention was divided into two main parts. There were designated areas for demonstrations in the latest technology. In another section independents pitched their products. The seminars were conducted in that area too.

Hannah scanned her program, then pointed to a

seminar on hosting talk shows. "Here's what I want."
Zack walked her over to the room.

"Wish me luck," she said.

He kissed her instead. "Have a good time, honey.
I'll meet you when you're through. Wait here or we'll
miss each other. There's someone I have to see."

She hated to leave him. "About your documentary?"

"No. You be a good girl and keep out of trouble."

"Yes, Daddy." Before she realized his intention,
she felt his tongue skim her lips. Automatically her
mouth opened to receive it.

"Nuts," he muttered, releasing her. "I wish we
were alone." She watched him leave, thinking how
alike their wishes were.

The main emotion Hannah felt as she sat through
the seminar was relief. Madge had covered most of
the same information as the instructor. She'd har-
bored the secret fear that there was so much left to
learn, she'd never make it through the first program. When the instructor selected her to be part of
a demonstration on technique, she didn't dare refuse.

Zack slipped into the room without Hannah knowing it. His meeting with Carl Beryl had resulted in
an excellent offer for a joint venture on a documentary about Denver, Colorado, from the 1800s through
to the present. It would mean hard work, but a
chance to be an independent himself. If he was fortunate and his documentary won an ACE, so much
the better. His future was looking bright. Morris
could replace him by moving Scott up and hiring
someone to fill Scott's slot.

His loins stirred as he looked at Hannah. The
lecturer was giving pointers on makeup and dress,

praising Hannah for her attire. Why not? She wore an electric-blue scarf, draped in a vee. Her dress was a pale peach sheer wool, setting off her luxuriant dark brown tresses. She had eyes that made people stop to look twice. She was beautiful, desirable, and soon to be his. What was more, he knew that beneath her usually calm facade beat the heart of a passionate woman.

Hannah caught sight of Zack as the session drew to a close. Her cheeks flushed with pleasure. She thanked the woman who'd given the session, then glided down the aisle to him. "It was wonderful," she said enthusiastically. "I want to pinch myself to make sure I'm really here."

"Let me do it instead. You've got some cute places I'd like to pinch."

He yelped when she did it first, then grabbed her hand. "I'm starved."

"What are you in the mood for?" she asked, walking rapidly to keep up with his long strides. He stopped with a jerk, swinging to face her.

"Don't ask," he said, smiling rakishly. "My mind's fuzzy around you."

She blushed again. Zack could win a prize as a romantic, she thought. No wonder the women at work fantasized about him. They were always filling her with stories of what they'd do if they got him alone. Which was what she was thinking at that moment. Simply being with him sent her desire to a fever pitch, and she couldn't wait until she was a part of him. Come what may, she'd have this night and the next.

They located one of the last empty tables in a

section reserved for fast-food kiosks. "We're lucky," Zack said. "There's a food convention going on, too, otherwise we'd eat in the cafeteria downstairs or grab a hot dog from one of the permanent stands. So, you've got your choice. American, Chinese, Italian, Greek, Swedish. What'll it be?"

Zack chose a turkey club on rye; Hannah ordered a tuna melt. He frowned at her selection. "The mayonnaise might not be fresh. Can't have you getting sick. You'll ruin Sarah's milk." He said it so matter-of-factly and with such concern for Sarah, Hannah couldn't get angry at his bossy ways. "All right," she said. "I'll have what you're having."

They lingered over lunch, enjoying the hubbub and commotion. Whenever people Zack knew wandered by, he made introductions. The conversations, touching on ratings, market share, rising advertising costs, and the coming ACE Award contest, fascinated Hannah. Thanks to Morris, Zack, Madge, and Scott, she understood more of this interesting profession.

Zack, ever aware of her, wasn't surprised when men lingered to talk. They were captivated by Hannah's looks, a natural beauty she never flaunted. Nat Edwards, a producer with one of the networks, strolled over with a soda in his hand. He accepted Zack's invitation to join them.

Nat was dressed in jeans and a blue sweatshirt with the logo *Make Love Not War*, and his sandy blond hair was cut in a fifties-style crew cut. Hannah mentally compared the two men. Zack was an ad for GQ in his tan slacks and matching sport jacket. Nat looked ready for a Beach Boys concert.

Zack told her about Nat's credits as a producer, adding, "Last season he had more hit shows on the air than any other producer."

She did a double take, and Nat smiled intently at her. He obviously knew the impression he made on people. Yet when he fired a series of questions at her, she began to understand that he was a man who left no stone unturned.

"Where have you been hiding?" he asked. "Are you in the business? I don't usually forget a face like yours."

Zack smoothly cut in. "Hannah and I work together."

"Doing what?" Nat ignored him, concentrating on Hannah.

She felt Zack's concern. "I'm just starting. I'm going to guest-host Madge Evan's show for a few weeks."

Nat's brows shot up. He was apparently impressed. "Once a year I try to hire Madge. I'm always hoping she'll relent and switch. If she's placing her trust in you, then you must have what it takes. Where's Madge going while you take over?"

Hannah glanced at Zack, and was grateful when he explained about Madge's health. Nat was genuinely sorry to hear the news. "I'll give her a call." Turning back to Hannah, he asked, "What have you done before?"

"Not much," she admitted, then corrected herself. "Nothing yet, actually."

"Then how did you get the job?"

Zack furnished the answer, again smoothing the way for her. "Hannah wanted to change fields. She was hired by Morris. She's been in training in a general sense to see where she'll best fit in. From the first, Madge suggested Hannah go on camera. She chose her for her replacement, and she's been coaching her."

Nat finished his soda. "Sounds like a Cinderella story. You show up, ask for a job, and then Madge Evans discovers you." He shook his head. "She must see a winner in you. Her show is too close to her heart for her to jeopardize the ratings. What sort of work will you be doing when she returns?"

"I don't know," Hannah replied honestly. "Whatever Zack and Madge feel I'm best suited for."

Nat pulled his wallet out of his pocket and handed her a business card. "We're always searching for new talent. Send me a tape of one of the shows. I'll have my staff look at it. We'll keep it on file in case something comes up. In this business, stranger things have happened." With a pat on Zack's shoulder, he rose. "See you, Matthews."

Hannah sat in shock. "Did he say what I thought he said, or did I dream that?"

Zack grinned. "Honey, there's nothing wrong with your ears. We both heard it."

"But he's such a baby."

Zack sat back laughing. "That *baby*, as you call him, carries a lot of power. He has an uncanny gift of knowing what the public wants. Welcome to the wacky world of show business."

Hannah's face revealed her incredulity. "Are most producers like him?"

"Are you kidding? He's one of a kind. He's good at everything but marriage. Nat's just gotten his third divorce. His logo is a personal message."

Hannah let out a puff of breath. "He must have started when he was ten."

As the afternoon drew to a close, Zack and Hannah left the center to check into their hotel. She was surprised to discover it was a well-known one that faced Central Park. As Zack spoke to the desk clerk she felt a fresh attack of nerves. Zack had said nothing about the sleeping arrangements. She wondered if the clerk could tell by her face that they weren't married. In a pretense of interest, she stared at the fresco ceiling, the potted plants, the Victorian furniture, anything to avoid the man's eyes.

When he was through checking in, Zack turned to her. "Don't worry," he said softly. "I booked two rooms."

She kept her eyes straight ahead, merely nodding at the information. But her mind was racing. Zack was expecting her to make the first move, and she couldn't. She just couldn't! Why hadn't she remembered that he'd said he wouldn't rush her? All day he'd been attentive, even boyishly aggressive, protective of her feelings with Nat. "I expected you to," she said stiffly.

"That's why I did it," he said, reinforcing her perception.

She allowed him to take her elbow and guide her to the bank of elevators. She stood quietly by his side as the elevator ascended to their floor. Halfway down the hall he stopped at a door.

"Here we are." He turned the key in the lock. "My room's next door."

She nodded and stepped inside. Her breath was taken away by the suite of rooms. The living room was a lover's delight, decorated in peach and aqua, with delicate and finely drawn botanical prints. On every table there were flowers: in cachepots and cut crystal, in porcelain bowls and fluted vases, and even floating atop water. There were roses, lilacs, violets, daisies, asters, and more. She clasped her hands to her mouth, her eyes wide with an emotion too strong to put into words.

In the center of the living room a table was set with Limoges dinner service, Waterford tulip stemware, a crystal wine decanter, and a bucket of chilled champagne.

Zack grinned and took her hand. "I know what you were thinking down there, Hannah."

She hid her face, not wanting him to see how she'd misjudged him. He gathered her in his arms. She breathed in his manly scent, felt his strong body sear her with its heat, as if she were wearing no clothing.

He led her into the bedroom, and she gasped in delight. The color scheme was a mass of blooming periwinkle and jonquil yellow: bedspread, shams, ruffles, and drapes. "I pictured you in a garden, Hannah. I asked for this room. I'd toured this hotel before when we filmed the landmark panel's effort to save it."

"But you signed for two rooms."

He nuzzled her neck. "For you, darling. In case you received a phone call from home. I didn't want you to be embarrassed if they reached you under my name. Unless you don't want me, I have no intentions of doing anything in my room except paying for it. This night and tomorrow is ours." He slipped his arms around her waist. "Are you hungry?"

She looked up at him, and what she saw in his eyes—the love, the hunger, the aching want—made the truth so easy to say. "Only for you, Zack. Only for you."

He crushed her to him, momentarily at a loss for words. It seemed as if he'd waited a lifetime for her. Tenderly, he touched her cheek, bringing her lips to his. His arms tightened around her, gathering her closer, pressing her to his chest, his hips.

Her body was soft, feminine, a perfect complement to his hard, muscular physique. She murmured something inaudible, as if it were too difficult for her to speak. He wanted this woman, yearned to make her one with him. Instinctively he knew she would never be loved the way he would love her.

Hannah stared into his eyes, enthralled by the fire in their depths. Here was the man who would wipe away the past. She had never been so aware of her need for him as now. This man—with his incredibly dark gaze, his kind concern for her and her child—this man made her heart leap.

Her lips parted, offering the moist gift of love. Smiling, she brought her mouth to his, tasting first the sweetness and then the heat. The miraculous, devouring, all-powerful heat. "I want you," she whispered. The words were smothered and swallowed by a moan as he robbed her of her senses, lifting her in his arms as if she were the most precious woman in the world.

Effortlessly, he carried her to the king-size four-poster bed his own pulse thundering in his brain, in his heart, deep within his very soul. Their hands searched, tore, flung off unwanted clothes, until at last they lay naked, their arms wrapped around each other as if even a scant breath of space between them was too much separation to bear.

Then Zack moved back, staring at her. Her hair lay in disarray on the pillow, a wealth of shimmering brilliance. She lowered her eyes and bent her knee, hiding that secret part of herself. He gently eased her leg back down. "No. I want to see you. All of you. Don't ever be shy with me, Hannah. Let me love you."

Reverently he showed her with his hands and lips his adoration. He caressed her face, her neck, the soft undersides of her breasts. No place was left unloved. He blazed hot trails, exploring her body everywhere, to the feminine nest that would receive him.

Hannah offered herself to him without restraint, glorying in the exquisite pleasure. His body became known to her, his weight familiar. She imitated his caresses, giving him the erotic pleasure he was giving her. They strained toward each other, transcending the present, catapulted into a world neither had ever known yet each had dreamed of. They were in a place of their own making, protected and nurtured by loving hands, worshipful lips, and passion beyond their belief.

Zack knelt beside her, his ardent gaze searing her, his finger skimming her inner thigh. The flowers vied with the heady fragrance that was Hannah. Her body was made for loving. He saw in her face, in her wondrous eyes, a mirror of his own emotions.

He took her breast into his mouth. She moaned, increasing his pleasure, his delight in her. He suckled the nipple, lavishing and lingering until he heard her cry out.

Hannah touched him, running hands mindlessly over his back, his firm haunches, his smooth buttocks. She traced endless patterns over his tantalizing body, then pulled his head up, her appetite for him surging. Never before had she been so aroused. She was too excited. Her appetite for Zack was all encompassing.

She pressed him back onto the bed, lifting her body to cover his. Leaning on her side, she kissed his chest, her hair a curtain of silk around them. Her marauding fingers found his rigid manhood, and a sense of power surged through her. A low, throaty chuckle escaped her as Zack writhed with pleasure. It was her turn to give him the ecstasy he'd given her. She blazed a trail with her mouth, down, downward.

He was going out of his mind, throbbing with urgency. "Hannah," he gasped, his hands reaching under her shoulders. Impatiently he dragged her up to shower her with kisses. Her mouth was swollen from his demands, his passion, his devotion.

For a moment he loomed over her, his dark hair damp, his eyes heavy-lidded, looking at the woman who in all the world was the one made for him. He raised her hips. A single, swift thrust and they were one, united with all the joy each offered the other.

Hannah cried out his name, arching her body upward. Her fingers dug into his hard muscles, her legs locked him in a fierce embrace. With his force, with his body, with his eternal soul, he poured his essence into her. "Darling," he whispered. "My sweet, sweet darling."

A star burned and formed, taking shape, hurtling them outward, away from their earthly confines. His mouth closed over hers as he exalted in the creation of their making. Hannah lost all track of self. He had shown her the universe and created a new world, wiping out all her past unhappiness. She was new.

Presently they floated back to earth, reveling in their discovery, murmuring secrets, words of praise. They slept, content and sated. The champagne waited among the bower of flowers. Hours later, locked in each other's arms, they stirred in their sleep, seeking and touching. They looked into each other's eyes.

And smiled.

Everything in the world had changed, and they had brought it about.

Zack nibbled Hannah's neck. She mumbled in her sleep. As his caresses continued she came slowly, deliciously awake, suspended in a sensation of swirling black velvet. "How long have you been up?" she asked, touching his face.

He turned on the Tiffany lamp near the bed. "Ever since you snored and woke me up."

She sat bolt upright, all sleep vanished. "I don't snore!"

"I know that," he said, throwing an arm around her waist, pinning her down.

"Then why did you say I did?" she persisted. Did

she snore? If she did, she'd die. She'd sit up the rest of the night rather than let him hear her snore. What could be more unromantic?

"Well, you do," he said. "A little."

She didn't trust the smirk on his face. Zack could be very playful. "How little?"

He trailed his fingers over her hip. "Very."

"Not even a little," she said, in no uncertain terms. "I have never snored in my life." She hoped.

He rubbed his foot along her leg. "Have it your way." She looked so sad he was immediately contrite and apologized.

"Then why did you say it?" she asked.

"I figured we were getting along too well. I wanted to see how you handled a fight. Besides, I wanted to wake you up."

"A fight. You want to fight? Okay, buster, you asked for it." In a blink of an eye, she was on her feet, aiming a pillow at his head. She scored a hit and a grunt. "Bull's-eye!"

"So the little lady wants to play."

She yelped, dashing over to the other side of the room, where they'd thrown a spare pillow onto a chair. Taking aim, she hurled it. "Tell me I snore, will you!" She ran to the far corner of the spacious room, shrieking and laughing.

"You snore."

"Do not." He scored one on her behind.

"We're going to get thrown out of here." She laughed, belting him in the face.

Zack dove to the floor, retrieving the feathered missiles she'd flung. He lunged for her, grabbed her by the waist, and held on for dear life. They were both hysterical. She struggled, but when he swung her around and kissed her to silence her, she surprised him by giving in immediately, pressing her breasts to his chest, her thighs to his legs. He made a thorough job of the kiss, but the second he let her up for air, she went on the attack, pushing him backward onto the bed.

Naked, she straddled him, looking to him like a glorious hoyden. "Give up?" she demanded, pummeling him. He tried to duck, but she found him. He was laughing uproariously. When he couldn't talk he pointed, kept pointing. "Now what?" she screeched.

"Hannah," he gasped, protecting his face. "Look at yourself in the mirror." The bed was opposite a gilt-edged beveled mirror.

Curious, she swung her head to see what he was laughing about. "Oh, my!" She started to giggle, then the giggle turned into a laugh and finally a roar. She was a sight. Naked as a jaybird, her limbs entwined with his, her hair flying in every direction, looking as if it had been wired for electricity. Her face was alive with happiness, her eyes burning with mischief, her cheeks flushed. She stuck out her tongue. "You're not much better," she said, refusing to give an inch. Exhausted, she slumped against him.

His hands roamed down her hips to the back of her thighs. With his legs he locked her in a vise.

"Did I really snore?" she asked.

"No, you silly goose." He was rewarded with a sigh of relief. He kissed the side of her neck, then angled his head to nip her breast. "Wanna make up?"

She kept her eyes tightly closed, enjoying the sensation. "What did you have in mind?"

He shifted his body. "Something will come to me."

She loved the touch of his bare skin, his legs with their coarser hairs on hers. She wrapped her arms around his neck. "Mmmm, this is nice."

"Nice good or nice terrific?" he asked, licking the soft spot below her ear.

"Nice terrific," she answered, arching her back.

His hand cupped her breast. "In that case you won't mind if I continue." His deep laugh let her know he'd have continued in either case.

"More," she whispered, reacting as she always did to the caress of his lips.

"Lots more," he agreed, nudging her legs apart with his knee, exultant as she writhed in ecstasy.

Afterward he held her close. "Nice good or nice terrific?"

"Keep trying," she purred, feeling feminine and totally wanton. "One of these times you'll get it right."

His answer was a highly satisfied masculine growl. Locked in each other's arms, they slept.

Hannah opened her eyes slowly, orienting herself to the splendid surroundings. Zack lay on his side, gazing at her. "You're up," she said, tugging the sheet to her chin.

"Now that beats all. We spent the night in glorious nakedness. All of a sudden you're shy."

"I can't help it. It's light out. The city's up." Even to her own ears, her response sounded ludicrous.

"That makes sense," he said, taking pleasure in teasing her.

Her pulse skipped. "Quit watching me. You're much too randy."

He propped himself up on one elbow. His hair was tousled from her fingers. There were traces of lipstick on his face. "Your wish is my command, madam. Would you rather I look at the flowers, or the walls maybe?"

Her eyes gleamed. He had the body of an athlete . . . and the stamina. She giggled. "It's just that I know what you're thinking."

He laughed. "*That* is the furthest thing from my mind." When she coyly lowered her lashes and bent her head to run her tongue over his stomach, he gasped. "Oh, hell, why not."

Seven

Hannah strapped on her leather sandals. Comfort won over fashion. "Why didn't you tell me the Javits Center is five city blocks long and three stories tall? The marble floors are beautiful, but they're murder on high heels. Every woman I saw wore sneakers, and I was tramping around in heels."

"Grouch, grouch, grouch. I like you in heels. There's something about the back of a woman's leg, the curve of her calf, that turns me on." Zack pressed his lips to her cheek. "Other parts turn me on too."

"Mmmm, that's nice." Her gaze swept over him. If it were possible to get more good-looking each day, Zack had the secret. "You're going to age very well."

"What brought that on?" he asked.

Suddenly she felt shy, as if all of her inner dreams, all of her deepest thoughts about the intimate moments they'd shared were written plainly on her face. She was overwhelmed by the realization that she'd taken a step on an unknown path. Engulfed by a sensory overload, she wanted to memorize the luxurious surroundings, take the images home. Everything had a special meaning now. The bottle of champagne nested in the silver bucket. The fluted glasses they'd used to toast each other. The table set with pale peach linen imported from Ireland, the single matching rose with its petals unfurled in the crystal light of day. The elegant bedroom, the pale peach satin sheets mussed from a night of intense lovemaking. The music from unseen speakers, and so much more.

She walked over to Zack, throwing her arms around his waist, resting her head on his chest.

"I'll never forget this room," she said softly. She ached exquisitely from his possessive lovemaking, but she was at such peace with herself she hardly cared.

"Neither will I." He kissed the top of her head. "We're going to be late. Duty calls."

"Aye aye, sir." She sprang away, pursing her lips in a moue. Finishing dressing, she fastened the belt on her cream-colored slacks, buttoned her matching long-sleeved shirt. Her hair glinted and swirled around her as she tilted her head to clip on her earrings. Behind her Zack stopped combing his hair. She glanced up, their eyes finding each other in the mirror. Her heart skipped a beat, and she leaned back, letting their bodies touch. "Okay?" she asked softly.

"More than okay." He grabbed a handful of hair. "I've never seen hair like yours. It has a life of its own, the way it moves so majestically."

She felt marvelous, light and free and giddy. "Now I have to brush it again," she chastised, but he knew better. He loved touching her. "You haven't stopped smiling all morning," she said.

He kissed her neck, lingering to inhale her scent. "Better than the roses," he said. "You're looking at an extremely satisfied man. How about you?"

"Well," she said, loving the feel of his body against hers, the firm muscles beneath his shirt, the manly scent that was his, "I'm not sure yet."

He swatted her bottom. "The last time you said that it took us another hour to dress."

She shook her head. "Can I help it if you're so slow?" He yelped, lunging for her, but she ducked out of his way.

"I'd better check up on Alexandra and Sarah. Alex'll probably think I've fallen off the face of the earth." Or something closer to the truth, she added silently. Soared up to heaven.

"Good idea." Zack followed her to the bed, tucking in his shirt and buckling his belt. He sat down to tie his shoelaces.

Alex answered on the fifth ring, giving her usual enthusiastic hello. "You just missed Phyllis. Of course Sarah's fine. Morris offered his assistance if I needed him. Said the family has to stick together."

Hannah cupped the receiver and related that news to Zack.

"Zack says that would be a major mistake, Alex. I take it you declined?"

"You take it right. Can you see Morris taking care of her? Listen, sis, I'm not prejudiced because I'm her aunt, but Sarah's got to be the best baby in the world. I'm teaching her to call me Mama."

"Don't you dare." Hannah knew Alex wasn't ready to settle down. To her Sarah was a toy. Give her a month on the job and she'd be tearing her hair out. "What did you do last night? Were you terribly bored?"

Alex hooted. "How could I be bored? In between lollipops I beat Scott at backgammon."

Hannah turned to Zack. "Scott was over last night." Zack's brows raised. "She beat him at backgammon."

"Ask her what color lollipop he gave her."

"I heard that," Alex called. "You can tell Zack I had my choice."

"You're kidding!" Hannah exclaimed, relaying the news. If Scott had given Alex a choice, he must have fallen hard. "What are you and Sarah doing right now?" She listened while her sister answered.

"So?" Zack asked, nudging her, impatient for her to continue the running commentary.

"Sarah's about to have a bath," Hannah said.

Zack wiggled his fingers, requesting the phone. "Hi, Alex. Yes, Hannah's doing fine. No, I'm not kidding. She saw Barbara Walters and hasn't been the same since. Listen, when you give Sarah her bath she likes to play with the frog I gave her. Of course in the water! Don't make the water too hot. You'll burn her tender skin. Oh, and remember not to get water in her ears. Use a cotton swab or the end of a cloth. Not soaking wet, either." He whispered to Hannah, "Your sister keeps breaking in. Is she always like this?"

Hannah's mouth was hanging open. If Zack could

only see the serious expression on his face. "I—I don't know."

He snorted and turned back to the phone. "Oh, and when you dry her, be sure to kiss her tummy and blow. She loves that. Okay, here's Hannah."

Alex was laughing when Hannah got the phone back. "Hannah, did you hear the list of orders he shot at me? You'd think he was the father of that kid instead of me being the blood relative. Is he for real?"

Hannah cleared her throat. Zack had no idea the effect his speech had had on her. He had spoken with such love and concern. Oh, yes, she thought, her heart thumping. "He's for real."

"Don't let him get away," Alex advised before hanging up.

"Well, she does like to have her tummy kissed," Zack muttered as he stood up. He grinned sheepishly when she stood, too, and wrapped her arms around his neck. His hands slipped down her back, holding her loosely at the waist.

Hannah languidly shifted her hips, rotating them. "And what does the mommy like to have kissed?"

He blew in her ear, sending tremors of longing radiating through her. "Mommy likes to have her tummy kissed too."

"Does it hurt to have a baby?" Zack asked as he lay on the bed watching her dress for the second time. They were going to be awfully late.

Hannah thought back to the night Sarah was born. Her water had broken while she'd been driving home from the store. Morris had arrived earlier that day, and she'd wanted to make a nice meal for him. She'd known that he and Alex worried. They had insisted that for the two weeks prior to her due date, Morris would be there the first week, Alex the second.

Morris had arrived loaded with presents for the baby. A football. A soccer jersey. A tennis racket. The list of useful gifts went on. She'd thanked him profusely for his thoughtfulness, kept the rattle out, and put the rest on a shelf in the closet. "Girls play football and soccer," Morris had assured her. Maybe when they learned to walk, she'd thought, but not before they crawled.

"It's hard to answer," she said to Zack. "Yes, it hurts, but once it's over, you forget it and just enjoy the life you've given birth to. Sarah was beautiful. She wasn't wrinkled or red like most newborns. She was pink, her head nicely shaped. She was perfect."

"Was Morris with you?"

She smiled. "After a fashion. Poor man. He arrived in town to do the honorable thing by his dead sister's child. And you know Morris. He's been a bachelor all his life. I doubt if he's ever held a baby, let alone helped give birth to one. No sooner did he arrive in California than he was volunteered. Literally."

Zack propped the pillow behind his head. "How was that?"

"My friend Sheila and I were partners in training at the Lamaze classes. She came down with the flu, so at the last minute she had to drop out. You can imagine how frantic I felt."

Unlike Hannah, Zack wasn't smiling. He was furious with her husband for not being there when she needed him.

"It's hard to picture Morris capped and gowned telling you to breathe."

Hannah chuckled. "He didn't. At the last minute he got the cold sweats. He was dying for a cigar. The nurse shooed him out before he fainted. Poor Morris. He was so embarrassed. Don't you dare tell him I told you. It's the thought that counts."

Zack pushed himself off the bed. He looked closely at her, his eyes filled with compassion. "If you were my wife, you'd never have gone through that alone." Hannah couldn't speak. She was too choked up.

As Zack and Hannah walked along on the Concourse Level, Hannah chattered away, telling him about the 100,000 square feet of skylights and the 864 miles of wiring in the Javits Center.

"You're a regular tourist, aren't you?" he teased.

"Well, don't you want to know about this place?" she asked.

"New Yorkers never ask questions. They take it for granted." She took him seriously, so he added, "I suppose you think the 230,000 square feet of terrazzo flooring is impressive too?"

She pulled up short. "You read the fact sheet, you faker!" When he didn't pause, she had to hustle to catch up with him.

"Of course I did," he said haughtily. "I promised Sarah I'd tell her everything we learned and what we did."

She laughed. "You do and I'll kill you!"

He gave her a quick, hard kiss as they parted. "I'll meet you upstairs in the Crystal Palace, say in about two hours. And don't pick up any strange men. You're mine!"

A hot thrill ran through her at his words. She knew he didn't mean anything serious or permanent by it, but it was fun to pretend. During the seminar her mind wandered and she had to keep forcing herself to stay alert.

Later, with time to kill, she decided to see the exhibits. Thinking of Madge, a fresh attack of nerves hit her. In a few days the fun and games would be over. She'd be Madge's replacement.

Butterflies fluttered in her stomach. She fell victim to the "What if's." What if after all her preparation she failed? What if Zack was disappointed in her and was too much of a gentleman to show it? What if Morris was sorry he'd hired her but was too polite to fire her? What if at that very moment, Madge was sitting at home, her hand wandering to the phone as she screwed up the courage to call her to cancel the whole thing? The list of "What if's" went on.

She took the escalator to Level Three, the Crystal Palace, and found a vacant seat in the lounge area. Picking up snatches of conversations, she realized most people were talking about ratings: low and high. She bit down hard on her lip, sure that within two weeks, *her* ratings would be discussed. You could fool some of the people some of the time, but you couldn't fool all of the people living in the 200,000 homes her live program would be beamed to. With great good luck, no one would be home, and if they were they'd all be tuned in to another station.

"Getting cold feet?"

Hannah looked up at the sound of the familiar voice. Nat Edwards, dressed as he had been the day before, sat down beside her. She was glad to see him, and let out a sigh. "Is it that noticeable?"

"I've been there," he said. "You're very good, Hannah. I took the liberty of watching you from the back of the room earlier this morning. When you were chosen to role-play with the lecturer, you were natural. Don't forget to send me a tape."

" 'Role playing' is right," she said worriedly. "It's the real McCoy that's got me scared out of my wits."

"If it helps, even the stars get stage fright. Does Zack know how you feel?"

"He's the one who's been holding me up. You can see the jelly I turn into given five minutes alone."

"We can't have you turning into jelly. Come on, let's get a drink. I'll tell you some fright stories and cheer you up."

"I can't believe you were ever nervous," she said, walking alongside him to the snack bar.

"Believe it. Barrels of antacid tablets are sold to actors and television people because of butterflies in the stomach." They got in line at the snack bar. "Am I cheering you up?" he asked, and told her about an actress who had parts in two soap operas in the days before tape. "The director tore his hair out, the other actors on the set almost died, because there was our lovely blond actress emoting on the set, crossing story lines of the two shows. The switchboard lines lit up for days."

Hannah's jaw dropped. She didn't see the humor. "Poor thing. Did she lose her job?"

Nat grew serious. "In a manner of speaking. I married her. It didn't work out, but we had a nice run."

"I feel better. Thanks for taking the time, Nat. I really do appreciate it."

He squeezed her hand. "You're welcome. By the way, I saw Zack before and congratulated him." He caught Hannah's blush. "So that's the way it is between you two. I wondered."

She couldn't let him think she and Zack were serious. Not once last night or that morning had Zack mentioned the word "love." They were simply two consenting adults.

"Please, it's not what you're thinking. We're just friends."

Nat ordered two soft drinks and a hot pretzel. He squirted mustard on it. "Order something else. Danish? Hot dog?" Hannah declined, preferring to save her appetite to eat with Zack.

They climbed the short flight of stairs to a plush lounge, found an empty table, and sat down.

Nat took a big bite of his pretzel. "Zack put together quite a deal yesterday with Carl Beryl. What with his documentary placing in the semifinals, I bet you two had a lot to celebrate. I just heard about it. So what do you think? Will the station be the same when he leaves?"

Hannah couldn't believe her ears. Too much! her mind screamed. The noise of the convention faded as she struggled to process the news. Why hadn't Zack told her he'd sent in his documentary, let alone placed in the semifinals? He hadn't mentioned anything about a Carl Beryl. Why? What was this marvelous deal that was worth a celebration? When was Zack leaving? Her heart pounded at his betrayal.

Or was it a betrayal? she thought dully. Where was it written that because they'd made love, she had a right to know his private affairs? She had no claims on him. He'd never forced himself on her. And he *had* told her he was meeting someone. He just hadn't gone into any details. But why hadn't he trusted her enough to share this news?

The answer was all too clear. Zack wanted to sleep with her. He knew her story and no doubt had decided that if she knew the truth it would put a crimp in his style. She might have said no.

His needs over her trust!

Hannah struggled to keep smiling, though she was beginning to tremble. Tears filled her eyes and she quickly drew out a tissue, pretending a sudden attack of allergies. Trying to be fair, she attempted to look at it from Zack's viewpoint. She'd known from the start he intended to move on to greener pastures. He was very talented, wanted more creative control in programming. He and Morris had differences of opinion, so it was only logical for Zack to branch out on his own if the opportunity arose.

So why couldn't she take this news in stride? Dope that she was, she'd let herself believe in fairy tales again. She composed her features, aware Nat was watching her with avid interest.

"Zack deserves to seek his goal wherever he can find it," she said. "If it means moving on, that's what he should do. I wish him the best of luck. The station will survive. None of us is indispensable."

"Very pretty speech," Nat said. "You won't mind if I don't believe all of it, do you?"

"I thought I saw you two from down there," Zack said, suddenly appearing beside them. "Believe all of what?" He slid into an empty chair beside Hannah. His smile said he was happy to be there. The arm around her shoulder and the gentle squeeze proclaimed ownership. Hannah tried to erase her pained expression.

"I've been looking for you, Zack," Nat said easily. "I spent today catching up on news, since my being here is mostly a formality."

"Formality?" Hannah asked. She wished Zack would stop massaging her shoulder. His thigh brushed hers.

"Yes. You know, show my face. Press the flesh. That sort of thing. It goes with the territory." He stood up suddenly and pumped Zack's hand. "Hey, Zack, you have some great news. Placing in the semifinals for the ACE is a feather in your cap."

"Who told you?" Zack asked quietly. He glanced at Hannah and their gazes locked. His worried, hers hurt.

"Carl," Nat answered. "He also told me about the production company you two are forming. It sounds great. What kind of specials do you plan to market?"

Zack cursed silently. He'd known since the previous day about placing in the semifinals, but hadn't wanted to tell Hannah. Not yet, not after he'd already told her it was a stepping-stone to his leaving. He'd wanted to break the news to her in private today, to tell her they'd still see each other, that he wasn't going to bow out of her life. Instead it had been thrown in her face like a dash of cold water. No wonder she looked so stricken. She was probably thinking he'd used her.

Distracted, Zack said, "Carl talks too much. We still have some things to work out. But we'll probably do sports to begin with. We can sell to smaller stations around the country. We have a few other things we want to branch into."

"Congratulations, Zack," Hannah said softly. "I'm very happy for you." Adjusting her chair out of his reach, she gave him her most radiant smile, then favored Nat with a similar one.

"I have some news too," she said. "Not as spectacular as yours, certainly, but news nevertheless. Nat heard me in a practice session today. He was very kind in his remarks. I'm going to send him a tape of one of the shows. As he says, you never know what a chance meeting can lead to. Maybe Nat and I will be working together some day."

Zack scowled. "Marvelous." He scraped back his chair. "Hannah, are you about ready to leave? We've got a long evening ahead of us."

"Oh, but I've changed my mind," she said brightly. Zack's closeness was nearly suffocating her. She'd come to New York on a dream and it was turning into a nightmare. "You go ahead. I'm not a baby. I'll be able to find my way around. Besides, I'm not going out tonight. I'd much rather go back to my room, take a bath, and order in." She glanced at Nat. "When Nat and I are through chatting, there are a few other people I want to see. I'll take a cab."

Zack started to say something, then clamped his mouth shut. After a moment he rose and shoved his hands in his pockets. "Fine with me. See you, Edwards."

As he walked away, misery engulfed Hannah. The fantasy was over.

"Whew!" Nat said. "When you get mad, you get even, don't you?"

She sat up straight, her spine not touching the back of the chair. "I don't know what you mean."

"I beg to differ with you," he said kindly, then let it go. "You know, ever since we met I've had the feeling I've seen you before. Have we ever met?"

She smiled at him. She liked his down-to-earth manner and was grateful to him for giving her time to regain her self-control. "You may have seen me at a function with my late husband, Larry Rivers. He was with your network in California."

The name brought the expected response. Nat's brows raised. "So you're Hannah Rivers. I was sorry to hear of your loss."

"We were separated," she said bluntly. "There's nothing to be sorry for. My last name is Morgan, not Rivers. If you knew Larry, then you also knew he played the field."

"I see," he said slowly. "Listen, about my telling you about Zack's news. Maybe I jumped the gun on that."

She spread her hands expressively. "There's nothing to apologize for. Zack's a grown man. He has an obligation to see that his career moves ahead. That's what he's doing."

Nat shook his head, frowning. "Then why do I have the feeling he wishes I'd never showed up?"

She shrugged, giving a half laugh. She was tired from holding back her feelings. "Because it's true."

"Zack's a good man."

"The best," she agreed, a shade too quickly to be believed.

Nat tore a plastic straw in two. It lay like a symbolic sign on the table. "Then go after him."

"No," she said pleasantly.

"Why not?"

Should she tell him of all the times she'd moved, she wondered, hoping at last to set down roots? Maybe to others her desire to stay in one place might seem foolish. All her life she'd lived a peripatetic existence. Her father, a civil engineer, had followed construction sites across the country. Hannah had never known if, when she came home from school, a moving van would be outside the door. Her mother never complained, or if she did it was done in private. "I love your father," she often told Hannah. "Someday you'll understand." It didn't happen for Hannah that way. Her "someday" was going to be different.

"I'm not a camp follower, Nat. To each his own. That's my new motto. It keeps me from getting hurt."

Nat crossed his legs, swinging his foot back and forth. "So here we sit. Two happy people. I'm a three-time loser. You had one unhappy turn at bat. I know Zack did too. What's being proved here? That you're the most independent woman on earth? Is saving face that important? Don't mix Zack up with Larry. I'm sure Zack intended to tell you when the time was right. Maybe he didn't want to jinx the deal. He's too fine a man for subterfuge."

"And you," she added, "are a valuable and true friend. He's lucky."

"I'd say you're both lucky if you give yourself a chance."

An hour later, Hannah wondered about their conversation as she emerged from the Javits Center and hailed a cab. She'd only just met Nat, yet felt as if she'd known him for years. His words rang true. Larry and Zack were as different as day and night. Assuming Larry had known his daughter, had even once seen her, she couldn't imagine him grabbing the phone to tell Alex how to bathe the baby, as Zack had done.

She found Zack in her suite, seated on the couch, a drink in his hand. "I thought I'd wait for you," he said.

"Oh?" She wasn't in the mood for a fight. It wasn't the same fun as throwing pillows at each other.

He rose and paced the room. Grim-faced, he stopped and stared down at her. "I'm sorry I didn't tell you."

"You don't owe me anything, Zack, so don't apologize."

He grabbed her by the arms. "Stop that, dammit! It's not often I make love to a woman all night long, only to have the door slammed in my face. And what's this business about you working with Nat?"

"Possibly working with Nat!" she flung back. His anger only served to incite hers. She threw her purse on the nearest chair and kicked off her sandals. "And I do sincerely congratulate you. Of course I'm not sure exactly what I'm congratulating you for, but take it anyway."

The shift in her attitude infuriated him. "Now that's clear as mud. Sit down, Hannah, and get this off your chest. There'll be no living with you otherwise."

All Nat's advice flew out the window. Ice flowed in her veins. "How dare you take that supercilious tone with me. I'm not one of the women at work who thinks the sun rises and sets in you. And we are not living together. I'm the one who sat there getting the surprise of my life this afternoon. How was I supposed to know you closed a deal, placed in the contest, and are about to quit? You'll admit that isn't the kind of news you were likely to forget. It's too bad you didn't tell me last night. Then we'd really have had something to celebrate."

He was furious and hurt and frustrated. "Good," he said, jerking her to him. He smiled thinly, and his breath heated her skin. "Why don't you strip? Since it's obvious to you I equate last night with my business deal, let's celebrate now." He thrust his hips forward, pressing his arousal against her. Tugging at her blouse, he ripped buttons off when he couldn't get them undone. "No sense in wasting it, is there?"

"You're disgusting," she hissed, fighting off his hands. She had never met a man who incensed her more.

"Am I?" he asked in a low, ferocious growl.

"You, Mr. Matthews, are a first-class heel. Last night was a mistake. Plain and simple. Or if it wasn't, it was plain-and-simple lust. You did me one favor.

You broke the ice for me. Now I'll be able to go on to bigger and better things—no pun intended!"

He moved then. As swiftly as a bolt of lightning, his head swooped down, his mouth covering hers, his tongue forcing its way between her lips. He smothered her with his mouth, kissing her savagely, taking her on a roller-coaster ride of emotions, sweeping her along on a surge of barely controlled energy. He held her and kissed her until she sagged weakly against him, hating herself and him for the power he had over her. And then the kiss changed, softened. His lips moved gently, giving and not taking. She clung to him, her breathing labored.

"Did you think I was leaving right away?" he asked.

"Aren't you?" Her lips were swollen from the bruising kiss. "Isn't that what this is all about?"

Sighing, he let her go and walked to the window. "What this is all about is us. Not an award or business. It's you and me and Sarah and seeing what we mean to each other. I've known a lot of incredibly spoiled girls who grew up into incredibly spoiled women. I suppose I wasn't looking in the right places. You, with your sweetness, your dedication to Sarah, and your willingness to work like a demon to prove yourself and make a better life for the two of you, attracted me. But I come with some baggage too. Like you, I've been through the mill."

He left hanging the unspoken sentence. *Let's not make another hasty decision either of us will regret.*

"When will you tell Morris?" she asked.

He returned to her and took her hand to lead her to the sofa. "Soon. It won't come as a surprise. There are some shows I'm still taping, others I'm obligated to. Even though the deal with Carl sounds pretty positive, we still have a few kinks to work out, regardless of what Nat heard. One major one is where we'll headquarter the company. Carl lost his lease on his place in Jersey."

"I see," she said quietly.

"Do you, Hannah? Did you think I'd leave you in the lurch just when you're starting your career?"

She looked down. It was exactly what she had thought.

"You don't know me very well, after all," he said sadly.

Glumly, she realized she didn't know herself very well either.

Alex met them at the door and reluctantly handed Sarah to Hannah's waiting arms. "Traitor," she mumbled to her niece. Hannah folded the baby close to her breast, kissing every exposed spot of flesh. "I missed you, punkin."

Alex beamed. "I've decided she can call me Auntie Alex and when she's older we'll fly away together."

"This child goes nowhere without her mother," Hannah said, hugging Sarah tighter.

"She'll leave you for the first handsome man to make a grab for her," Zack said, and bent down to kiss Sarah. Her eyes lit up. She gurgled, her chubby hands reaching for him. "See what I mean?"

He lingered at the door a minute, his gaze briefly holding Hannah's. "See you tomorrow." After he left, Alex, Hannah, and the baby lay on Hannah's bed.

"Too bad Zack couldn't stay for dinner," Alex said.

Hannah sighed and got up to put her clothes away. "I imagine he's got some work to do."

Alex thumped the bed, bouncing a laughing Sarah. "So tell me already. Don't keep me in suspense."

"About what?"

Alex rolled her eyes. "Everything. Do you know how many lollipops I ate? The dentist is going to love me."

Hannah scooped up a blouse and hung it on a hanger. "When are you going to learn to stop asking personal questions?"

"Oops! Pardon me. Do I hear a note of discontent in your voice? Is this the sister I sent away with stars in her eyes? The one I spoke to on the phone and all I heard in the background was heavy breathing? A man's heavy breathing, I might add?"

"Oh, Alex," Hannah cried softly. She gazed around the room. It wasn't made with Frette linens. Her bedspread wasn't a flower garden. Her bathroom didn't have customized Italian marble. There was no handsome Swedish cabinetry to conceal a state-of-the-art remote-control television, VCR, and stereo system, or a fully stocked bar with crystal glasses. The only flowers in the room were on the wallpaper.

"Zack's leaving."

Alex sat up. "Is he going to Siberia?"

"No, silly."

"Then I fail to see the problem."

Hannah unbuttoned her blouse to nurse Sarah. "I said some things I'm sorry for. You should have heard me. I sounded like a shrew, a wife bent on angering her husband, when all the time Zack was wonderful. I was hurt because he withheld some very important personal news from me."

"What was that?"

"He's got a chance to win an ACE. That's the cable industry's award, like the Oscars. And he and another man are setting up their own production company."

"That's marvelous. But why didn't he tell you?"

"I'd rather not go into that. He said he was planning to. The problem is, out of sight, out of mind. Zack and I barely touched the surface of getting to know each other."

"I'll be happy to fly you wherever you want to go, so long as Zack's at the other end of the flight."

"That's very generous of you. There's only one small item missing. Nothing was said about a permanent relationship. Zack and I went to New York. We had some fun. Now it's back to work. Period."

Alex gazed at her with dismay. It was obvious to Hannah that Alex had dreamed up a happy ending for her, and had been hoping for an announcement.

"You're in love with him, aren't you?" Alex asked. Hannah gulped back a sob. "That bad, huh?"

Hannah shook her head. "I thought I was so grown-up. So with it. I was going off to New York on an adventure. Instead I fell in love and I'm miserable."

Eight

The following Friday was Hannah's big day, the moment of truth, the culmination of the hours of preparation with Madge and Zack. Inside the control room, Scott, Madge, and Morris waited in tense silence as the operator of Camera One cued Hannah to begin speaking. Zack, silently rooting for her, was a bundle of nerves.

Today's telecast was live. Zack did that once a month with the "Focus On" show to give it immediacy. Beyond the long window separating the control room from the set, Hannah appeared calm, cool, and collected, dressed in an off-white dress with a brightly colored scarf. The effect was fabulous. Her lips were painted a bright but not gaudy red, the shade chosen with care to keep the audience's attention on her face. Her hair was pulled back from her face, emphasizing her eyes. She'd played with various styles, recalling Dolores Farley's problem when her long hair brushed against the mike. Out of camera range, but visible to her anxious friends on the preview monitor, she twisted the script in her hands.

Morris viewed the monitor. Hannah's eyes were huge. "She's scared."

"Quiet, Morris, you'll jinx her." Madge sat down next to Scott. Her color was high and she cleared her throat often. Her husband was waiting outside the control room for her, not wanting her to drive home alone.

Zack cued Scott for the countdown, keeping his thoughts to himself. Morris knew his plans, was aware that Carl would be calling anytime and he'd be leaving. Zack missed Hannah. Since their return they hadn't had any private time. He missed holding her, loving her, playing with her, discussing . . . what? Their future?

Alex had left town on Monday. She'd stopped by the station to say good-bye to Scott, then had sought out Zack in his office. "Zack," she'd said. "Hannah's been through a lot in her young life. Maybe I'm out of line butting in, but I'd appreciate it if you didn't jerk her around."

He'd gotten angry, hating her choice of words. Yet underneath the rather crude way she'd expressed herself was the real love Alex had for her sister and Sarah. He couldn't argue with that.

"I won't," he'd said curtly, ending the conversation. But she'd set him to thinking about his goals. They hadn't changed, yet he was changing. He wanted to talk to Hannah about it, and at the same time was afraid to. She was distant, and she told him it was due to the pressure of work. He didn't buy that.

He knew her too well. Intimately, the way lovers of many years knew the rhythm of each other's bodies and thought processes. She was keeping him at arm's length. Exactly what did he want?

He wanted to make documentaries and have control over his creative life. He wanted to make love to Hannah and not make promises he wasn't sure he could keep. And Hannah was probably backing off for the same reason.

Babs McCauley on Camera One thrust out her finger.

Hannah sat straight, looking into the camera. "Good afternoon, and welcome to 'Focus On.' My name is Hannah Morgan, and it will be my pleasure to be your hostess for a few weeks while Madge Evans takes a long-overdue holiday. Our topic today is the environment, and our guest is Frank Able, owner of *Ables*, the fastest-growing fast-food restaurant chain in this state." She smiled, then continued. "Mr. Able, I understand that you now have over a hundred restaurants and plan on opening another hundred and fifty within the next five years. That's quite an accomplishment." She paused, letting him enjoy the compliment.

Frank Able nodded. "It will be good for the state. We plan on employing an army of helpers."

"For minimum wage," Madge muttered. "I never liked that man. He's too arrogant."

Zack breathed a sigh of relief. The stiffness in his shoulders eased. He hadn't realized how tense he was until he heard Hannah's introduction. He'd tried and failed to set aside his personal feelings, worrying like an anxious father over her debut. Her voice was strong, and as she and Able got into the interview, grew stronger. She stopped fidgeting with her hands.

"She's doing fine," he said as Morris looked to him for confirmation. Morris beamed.

Madge didn't say a word until the commercial break, then broke into a smile. "Told you! Can I pick 'em or can I pick 'em?" She punched Morris's arm. "Now I can go to the hospital in peace, guys."

"Will you look at that," Zack said. Hannah was reaching over to pat Able's hands, reassuring the man that he was doing fine. "She sounds like an old pro."

On the set, Hannah resumed her questioning. The script lay on her lap, but she'd practiced it so often, she scarcely needed it or her cue cards.

"You're a fortunate man, Mr. Able, owning a chain of fast-food restaurants."

He nodded. "One hundred and soon to be more," he reminded her.

"And you're an avowed environmentalist."

"It's irresponsible not to be," he said emphatically.

"Well then, Mr. Able, what thought have you given to packaging?"

"To packaging?" he repeated, nonplussed.

"Yes. Can you tell us why your restaurants disregard the environment? Surely you don't need all that plastic packaging?"

"What's she doing?" Morris snapped. On the preview monitor Frank Able's hands were fisted.

"My company," Able said stiffly, "has spent thousands of dollars studying packaging."

"I'm certain," Hannah said sweetly, "for every study

there's another that says something else. Why, when cigarettes were first advertised, they were thought to be healthy, the perfect relaxant for harried women, especially mothers. *Studies* now show otherwise."

"Cue up a commercial," Morris barked.

"You do and I'll never come back," Madge said impassively. "I want to see where she's heading with this."

They glowered at each other for several seconds, then Morris let out a breath. He nodded to Zack, who wasn't about to go to a commercial anyway.

"She's disregarding the script," Morris muttered. "No one in television likes surprises."

"Leave her alone, Morris," Zack said. "If you yank this now, you'll crush her. I won't let you do that to her. She's more important than a lousy show."

"You won't let me . . ." Morris rubbed his chin, then he smiled. He clapped Zack on the shoulder. "You're the boss, Zack. Let's see what my niece is made of."

"Mr. Able," Hannah was continuing sweetly, "with all the money you've spent on studies, why do you continue to use nonbiodegradable packaging?" Before he could recover, she added, "In fact, I've often wondered why a person ordering food to be eaten in the restaurant has to have it packaged at all. Why wrap it in those individual cartons? The amount of paper wasted, which comes from trees, is abominable. When we indiscriminately cut down trees we endanger the environment. The loss of trees harms the ozone, and that leads to the greenhouse effect, with possibly catastrophic results due to the raising of the temperature. Even our oceans could be affected, endangering some species of fish that only live in cold waters. We're really all connected, aren't we? In the food chain, I mean, which of course is your business."

Morris made a strangled sound while Zack cheered her on. Madge whooped.

Able swallowed hard, glaring at Hannah. "My restaurants use packaging to maintain cleanliness. I'm concerned about the health of live human beings!"

Hannah dipped her head to hide a smile. "Of course you are," she said softly, giving the impression of being apologetic, yet leaving the audience to question why he wasn't concerned about animals, water, air quality, and how important protecting all of the environment was to human existence.

In a compelling voice, she offered a counterargument. "Most restaurants bring the food to the table on a plate. The steak isn't packaged separately from the potatoes and the string beans. Do you eat your food at home in separate containers, Mr. Able?"

Scott hooted. Madge clapped her hands. Zack wanted to run down and kiss her. Morris scowled, intently eyeing the monitors. Able was looking apoplectic.

"Do something, Zack," Morris said fiercely. "Able's one of our sponsors. Hannah's murdering him."

Madge tapped Morris's arm. "I told you I'd walk. I don't need this job and you know it. That little girl down there has got 'star' written all over her. What did you expect her to do? Give him a free endorsement? Break her and I personally will send this tape to Nat Edwards. He phoned me last night and we spoke about Hannah. He likes her. Think about it,

Morris. You're the one who gave her a start. You could be the big winner in this."

Zack's heart was bursting with pride. Hannah had broken, if only for one program, Morris's long-standing rule never to get into a controversial matter without his express approval. Which was a joke, since everyone knew he wouldn't approve. So why, with all she had at stake, was Hannah doing this?

She was smiling confidently into the camera, ready to end the show. "Concerned businessmen like Mr. Able will save money while saving the environment," she said. "Ladies and gentlemen, and children, too, Mr. Able"—she smiled brilliantly at him—"and I would appreciate your comments. He is a forward-minded businessman, interested in the environment, as all of you are. There isn't an endless supply of clean water and clean air. We're asking you to phone the station and let us know your views on packaging. Do you want it eliminated when you plan to eat in the restaurant, or not? Let us know. Call in. Help Mr. Able." She gave the number. "Thank you. This is Hannah Morgan wishing you a pleasant day." The monitor went to black.

"Dammit, Zack," Morris shouted, "she editorialized. Madge, were you behind this?"

Madge smiled. "I wish I were. Morris, shut up for once in your life and realize what that woman is doing for this station's ratings. I bet my bottom dollar the response she gets will bring other sponsors on line. The hottest topic in the country today is the environment. Now be quiet. I want to remember all of it so I can dream about it in the hospital."

Hannah sat back, shaking. Her feet didn't seem to

be able to stop bouncing. Her fingers were tearing the script into shreds. In the seat opposite her, Mr. Able, a portly, balding, middle-aged man, wiped his horn-rimmed glasses. He stood up and seared her with an angry glare.

"You'll hear from my lawyers, young lady. I didn't come on this stupid show to ruin my reputation! Where do you come off telling people to call and tell me what to do? Morris!," he shouted, turning to rush up the stairs.

Glumly, she watched him wag his finger under Morris's nose. She couldn't hear her uncle's answer, but his arm was around Able's shoulder as he escorted him to the hall.

What had she done? She'd taken a terrible chance, all because Able had riled her. She'd followed Madge's script, until Mr. Able insisted he was an evironmentalist, irritating her when she knew whales were dying because they were unable to digest the plastic plates dumped into the ocean, and birds choked because plastic got caught around their necks. Madge! Oh, God, she'd let her down.

She stared around the studio. How could she think she belonged there? Black wiring snaked across the floors, attached like endless umbilical cords to cameras. The walls were drab concrete, and a jagged crack marred the far wall. The place could use a coat of paint, a change of decor. She wondered if prison walls were this ugly. Babs and the other camera operator rolled the Sony's to the side. She mumbled a halfhearted "Thank you" and wasn't surprised when each left hurriedly. They didn't want to witness her firing.

The door from the control room opened. A tremor made her knee twitch. She licked her dry lips. It was time to face the music, and from somewhere in her she tried to summon the reserves to do just that. This wasn't an old movie where the poor heroine suddenly saves the town and lives happily ever after. Those days were long gone. Dully, she raised her eyes and slumped farther into her seat. They were coming for her, Zack in the lead.

Zack eased into a chair, bringing it close to hers. He covered her shaking hands and kissed her cheek, not giving a damn what Madge or Scott thought. She needed reassurance, and if Morris came in there and dared yell at her, he'd punch him. Hannah had accomplished what no one else had the guts to do. She'd taken a stand on an important issue, let the world know it, and asked viewers to give their opinions.

He spoke in soothing tones, purposely avoiding the issue at first. "Hannah, you were marvelous. Your voice was strong, your delivery faultless. You even had the timing down to the second." She looked as if she were ready to break into little pieces. "I don't think that could happen twice in a million shows."

He put his arm around her. "Honey, would you mind telling me what happened, why you deviated from the script?"

Hannah gulped. Explaining to Zack felt so natural, so right, as if they were having an ordinary conversation and she was making her point. "He was wrong. I had to say something."

"Go on," Zack urged, knowing there was more.

She clutched his hands. "I've been to his restaurants. You should see all the paper and plastics they use that aren't safe for the environment. I mean, Sarah has to grow up in this world." She gazed at him, silently begging for understanding.

"Well, I'll be damned!" He hugged her. "My little crusader. Do you hear that, people? Hannah was angry. She was worried about Sarah's future. That's why she did it." He rose, giving Madge his seat.

Hannah took one look at her and felt like crying. Where did she come off ruining Madge's show? And Morris! He'd hated her, and she couldn't blame him. He'd given her a chance to make something of herself and she'd ruined it.

"Oh, Madge, I'm so sorry. I shouldn't—"

"Hush," Madge interrupted. "Is this the fearless interviewer? The mother who wants to make a better place for all of us? I'd say this is a cause for celebration, not a funeral dirge."

Hannah knew they were trying to make her feel better, but the fact was, Morris wasn't there. She knew what that meant. "I let you down, Madge. I'm sorry, Zack, Scott. I don't know what got into me. I lost my cool. I'll leave. Babs can do the show."

"Babs will do nothing of the sort," Madge said. "She's on camera, where we need her. You started this and you're going to finish it. Personally, I could have kissed you. Frank Able's known as the Garbage King of Paxton. I admit your style is unorthodox, but what the heck. It had to be said."

"You're not angry?" Hannah searched everyone's calm faces. Scott handed her a red lollipop. "For courage," he said.

"What we need to plan," Zack said, "is damage control."

Hannah blanched. "Mr. Able said he'd get his lawyers after me. I ruined his reputation."

"Bull," Zack said succinctly. "Frank Able isn't going to sue. He was just threatening you. After all, you did give him an unexpected jolt. I'll talk to him and see what I can do."

"I already did," Morris said, joining them. He wasn't smiling. "Hannah, you took quite a chance there. If I wouldn't let Zack do shows that I thought would raise the hackles of sponsors, what makes you think I'd let you?"

"Now see here," Zack said, throwing himself between a stricken Hannah and her uncle. "She doesn't deserve that. Hannah's never done this before. She reacted naturally."

Hannah put her hand on his arm. There was no sense in his getting in trouble when she was to blame. "No, Zack. Morris is right. I resign."

"Oh, no, you won't!" Morris boomed. "You can't resign and I'm not firing you!"

"But . . . but . . . I brought trouble down on your head. Able's threatening to sue. If I leave he'll be satisfied."

"Well, I won't." Morris pointed a finger at her. "Listen, in the last ten minutes the switchboard's been lit up like a Christmas tree. First off, everyone's saying good for you and they want to know all about you, so I guess we'll have to do a short segment on you.

"Secondly, they're angry, and when people are angry a good television reporter milks a story. We're going to do a follow-up, and this time you're going to have statistics to back up your claims—none of this generalized-conclusion stuff. Heck, I bet you didn't know the Governor has formed a task force to study this very problem in our state. Or that they've found an autopsy that rare gray whales have died when balloons get caught in their throats." He rubbed his hands together. "Zack, get on this. I want you and Hannah to have a list of guests on my desk Monday morning. If you have to work this weekend, do it."

For a moment no one spoke. They were all in shock. Was this Morris talking? "Yes, sir," Zack said finally.

Morris sent him a sly smile. "And furthermore, Zack, this'll make a heck of a documentary. Any man who places in the final's for an ACE Award can do a superior job showing the growing pollution problem and its cost to the quality of our life. What do you say?"

Zack was stunned. He looked at Hannah, who was smiling at them both. "Yes, boss."

"Do you mind telling us what brought about this change?" Madge asked, her curiosity on overdrive.

"Not at all," Morris said expansively. "No one threatens my family. Able cheats at golf, too. I happen to know he doesn't give a damn about anything but money. Hannah's right. Pollution control is everybody's business. Can't have Sarah's lungs hurt, can we?" He kissed a stunned Hannah. "Gotta call my lawyers. Able better not start with me. I'll take a full-page ad out. No one will play golf with him."

"I think I'm going to be sick," Hannah said after

he left. The excitement was getting to her. Her hands shook.

Madge rose, wagging an imperious finger at her. "You don't have time. Zack and you have your work cut out for you. Besides, never let it be said I'd allow you to steal my thunder on two fronts. Scott, hand me a lollipop. I want green, and don't tell me today's red!"

Scott handed her a medley of colors. "In case you change your mind." He kissed her cheek. "You're all right, Madgie."

"Quit calling me Madgie, young man. Alex told me you can't play backgammon worth a hoot. I suggest you practice or the next time she comes here she'll trounce you good."

He chucked her under the chin. "Yeah. Who'll practice with me? You?"

She smiled. "Wait a week after the operation. I should be in shape by then. Now take me to my husband before he gets jealous and challenges you to a duel."

Finally alone with Zack, Hannah looked at him and for the first time felt the world floating back into place. She'd missed him desperately. She heard the pounding of her heart and wondered if he did too. What was it about him that set her on fire? It wasn't just his good looks, although she was proud to be seen with him. It was more than that. He had a quality of caring that she'd never get enough of. For a person who tended to give more than she received, she knew that trait endeared him to her more than anything else.

"I don't care if you're bald," she breathed.

"I don't care if you have a mustache," he said solemnly.

They moved into each other's arms at the same moment. Zack crushed his lips onto hers. "I've missed you. I've missed holding you, being inside you."

She buried her face in his neck. "Shhh, someone will hear you. The mikes—"

"Are off."

"You look wonderful," she said, admiring his beige wool sport jacket and light flannel trousers.

"So do you. We can't help ourselves. We're two gorgeous people. Hannah, I respectfully request the honor of asking you and your daughter to accompany me on a date."

She looped her arms around his neck. "She's too young. Besides, I don't share." She saw he was serious. "Where to?"

"WBC has a yearly picnic for all its employees. It's a way to say thank you and have fun. The crew organizes it and there are prizes for all sorts of things. Everyone gets into the spirit of it. It's a week from Sunday. It'll be good for you and Sarah. There's basketball, boccie ball, horseshoes, hot dogs, hamburgers, and more."

She slid her fingers into his hair. "Isn't Sarah a little young to play those games?" she teased. "As for the hot dogs, you know what she eats." Her smile was all feminine, full of wiles and temptation.

He groaned, pulling her roughly against him, leaving no doubt of his desire. His hands trembled with the force of it. "We could let Morris bring her, then you and I could stay home and play our games. What do you say—will you go with me?"

She rocked back in his arms, tilting her head. "You do realize this means all the other women will be jealous. The Heartthrob is actually dating some-one from the office."

"They should know what else he's done." He kissed the corner of her mouth, then pressed his lips on hers in a passion-filled kiss. She raised on tiptoes to feel the rock-hard length of him. "Can we go home now?" he whispered.

She touched his hair, caressed his face. She wanted him as much as he wanted her. "I thought you'd never ask. Morris wants us to be ready by Monday. I haven't the faintest idea what we'll do all weekend, do you?"

He left a trail of kisses on her throat. When she purred, he bit her ear. "Morris is a stickler for de-tails. I know you want to make a good impression."

His hands covered her breasts. "Mmmmm. A good impression. Yes, oh yes."

His lips barely moved from her mouth. "We might be busy all weekend, what with one thing or another."

She closed her eyes and dreamed. "I certainly hope so."

Nine

They made love on the living room carpet. They made love in the shower. They made love on the bed. Zack was determined to make love in every room of the house.

"I never want you to go into a room without thinking of me and how we are together. I want you to think about us when you're talking to a stranger or a friend and all of a sudden you remember how I kissed you. What we did."

She didn't need to be told. She'd carry Zack in her heart forever. Tired, they fell into a deep satisfying sleep, awakening to the sounds of birds twittering in the elm tree outside the window.

"Sarah's hungry," Hannah said, starting to rise. "I have to feed her."

Zack stayed her with a kiss, then rolled lightly to his feet. "Let me bring her to you. Stay in bed and rest a while." He padded into the nursery. From her room Hannah heard him talking to Sarah, telling her she'd be with her mommy as soon as she was nice and dry. When he brought the infant in, she was tucked under his arm like a sack of potatoes, laughing. The moment she was in her mother's arms, though, she was all business.

Zack lay down on the bed next to them, listening to the gentle sucking sounds, watching her chubby fingers knead. "That has to be the most beautiful sight in the world."

Hannah glanced up, and the look in his eyes made her wonder how she'd get along without him. He filled her days and nights, and soon he'd be gone. And still they didn't talk about it.

Later Zack helped Hannah make breakfast, but he had trouble following the conversation. He'd received an unexpected phone call from Carl Beryl Thursday night. Now, when he didn't want it to happen so soon, it looked as if he'd be leaving quicker than he thought. Carl had set up meetings with Denver historians, important meetings if the script was to be written with authenticity, yet Zack wished he had more time to sort out his feelings.

There was no doubt that he was in love with Hannah, but what he couldn't resolve was whether it would be fair to ask her to pick up stakes and drag her baby across half the United States, only to pick up stakes again for the next job. He'd be traveling a lot following assignments. Hannah had been through that once. He knew what having her own home meant for her and Sarah. Hannah needed roots.

"Do you think Morris was serious about our working on a documentary?" she asked as he bit into a crisp strip of bacon they'd cooked along with scrambled eggs.

"You look like you're twelve," he said, a faint smile curving his mouth. She wore a blue jumpsuit, her face was scrubbed so clean it shone, and her hair tumbled down her back. His gaze was on her face, but his mind was on her body.

"Sir," she said with an impish grin, "twelve is a bit young, don't you think? Make it thirteen. And if you wouldn't mind answering a child's question, answer mine."

Sunlight was streaming in the window, shimmering in Hannah's hair. Zack was content just to watch her and not talk about business. Still, he answered her question. "I've never known Morris to kid around when it comes to business."

She nodded. "The phone calls turned the trick. They were overwhelmingly in favor of getting rid of all that plastic and paper cartons. Do you think Able will sue? After all, he isn't the only fast-food owner."

Zack refilled his coffee cup and topped off hers. "I doubt it. He'd only get bad press, and he doesn't want that. Being against the environment is like being against the flag and apple pie, to say nothing of mothers."

She breathed a sigh of relief. "Good. Otherwise I'd be begging Nat Edwards for a job."

He put down his knife and fork, amazed at the jealousy ripping through him. "You could come and work for me after we finish this project. We've already proven we can work together."

Hannah wished he hadn't said anything; then she could have imagined whatever she wanted, played the scene the way she'd dreamed. Why couldn't Zack use the forbidden words? "Love and marriage." Sadly, she realized that much as he liked being with her and Sarah, it wasn't enough. The mere concept of marriage was anathema. Zack protected his freedom.

She rose so he couldn't see her face. "I can't do that, Zack. You don't know where you'll be, and I need to give Sarah a stable home. I'm not a camp follower anymore." There was nothing more to be said without discussing marriage—a taboo subject.

She lost her appetite.

So did he.

"Have you heard how Madge did in the operation?" Hannah asked Morris Monday afternoon, when she and Zack presented their proposal to him. "The last time I called she still wasn't out of recovery."

Morris scanned the list of names they'd drawn up. "I spoke with Bill a little while ago. The doctor said it went well. They're waiting for the pathology report. As soon as he knows anything he'll call us. He knows we're family."

Morris set the proposal down and looked up at them, all business. "Frank Able's not going to sue. His PR man convinced him he should 'lead' the crusade by either dropping the paper wrapping or the plastic plate when serving any food to be eaten in the restaurant. When he showed him the savings, Able agreed, dollar signs softening his anger at WBC. He wasn't thrilled." Morris chuckled as he remembered the tale the public-relations man had told him. "Especially when Al Havermeyer, who happens to be our PR man, too, immediately drew up plans to reinvest the money in advertising. Frank," Morris said gleefully, "got skunked!"

For the next half hour they discussed the format of Hannah's next show. It was to be a discussion with the Governor, if he could fit it into his schedule, or his designee. "His office will get back to us later today," Zack said. "It seems the Governor's wife heard the program. This is her pet interest."

Morris gave him back the proposal. "Good work. So." He rubbed his hands. "How are you two getting along?"

Zack recovered first. He and Hannah were getting along famously—as long as they avoided certain off-limits areas. "Fine. As you can see from the overview, Hannah's contributions are equal. She's the one who contacted the Governor's office and the schools."

"That's not important, Zack," she demurred. "It's a joint effort. They're sending the minutes of meetings the Legislature has held the past several months to discuss changes in state law. I understand balloon launching is being done away with in schools."

"Do the kids mind?" Morris asked.

"Not at all," Hannah said. "According to one school principal I spoke with, once the children understood the importance of saving animals, they got into the swing of it. They came up with their own ways to contribute. They've drawn posters, even written plays. We're going to feature a group on one of our shows. It's time children were spotlighted for the good they do. All we hear about is the bad."

"What do you think about that, Zack?" Morris asked.

"I agree," he said, smiling at Hannah. "We live in a world we must protect."

"Have you made arrangements for Sarah so you can go to the picnic Sunday, Hannah?" Morris asked, changing the subject again.

She glanced shyly at Zack. "Zack thinks I should bring her. Would it be all right?"

"Bring her, by all means," Morris said. "Everyone brings family. Wait until the girls see her."

His words about family registered on both Hannah and Zack. Although they'd spent the entire weekend together, neither had said anything about being a family. Family meant marriage, to Hannah's traditional way of thinking.

Zack caught up with her later, after speaking with Carl on the phone. "Carl moves fast. He's got the documentary lined up and paid for."

She knew she should be happy for him. "Where did he rent space?"

"He'll come up with a place." Zack didn't tell her how soon he'd be going. He had to find Morris and tell him first.

Morris ducked into the control room at the end of the day after Hannah was finished taping that day's "Focus On" show. She'd done well. Her nerves were under control. When she didn't dwell on Zack's leaving, she managed.

"Come have a soda with me," Morris said. He brought her back to his office and closed the door. His office reflected his varied interests. On the walls were commendations from civic groups and the Better Business Bureau. There were framed letters from publishing executives. Hannah read one.

"When did you leave publishing, Morris?"

"About ten years ago. I think about it still."

She turned. "Oh? How come?"

"I don't know. There's a different kind of excitement to it. A craziness that I miss." He sounded wistful. "Who knows? One of these days I might give it another whirl. I still own the company. There are good men running it, but one wants to retire."

Hannah thought that both Zack and Morris wanted to be doing something they considered more challenging, even though what they were doing now seemed impossibly complicated to her. She sat down and pulled the tab on her soda.

"Are you in love with Zack?" Morris asked bluntly as she took her first sip.

"Come now, Morris. You didn't ask me in here to discuss my private life, did you?"

"As a matter of fact, yes I did. I'm your nearest blood relative now that Alex has flown off. We worry about you. So tell me. Are you in love with Zack?"

She smiled weakly. Morris was capable of sheer stubbornness, clinging to a subject until he got the answer he wanted. How could she lie anyway? She'd been falling in love with Zack ever since she met him. When he turned around to speak to someone and she watched the play of muscles in his back. When he folded his arms and leaned his weight on one hip, reminding her of a lazy cat. When he grinned at her with a knowing, intimate look until she blushed furiously and had to look away. When he was silhouetted against the midday sun and looked like a Greek god. When he held her hand and told her not to worry about being sued by Frank Able.

When he bathed and played with Sarah. So many times . . .

She avoided her uncle's piercing gaze. "It doesn't matter whether I am or not. Zack wants to try his wings. I'd never do anything to clip them."

"Spoken like a true wife. In the olden days."

"What? What do you mean?"

"I mean, dear child, a man who is worth having is worth fighting for."

Where had she heard that before? "You sound like a man I met in New York."

"Nat Edwards," Morris said, nodding at her startled expression. "When a fancy producer/director calls me to ask me to send him a tape of your interview with Able, I figure it's time to snoop. Apparently he's interested in you and that particular show."

"But how did he hear about it?"

"Beats me. Let's get back to Zack."

The ticking of the clock was the only sound in the office as Hannah framed her answer.

"I won't try to stand in Zack's way," she said at last. "It wouldn't be fair. He wants to have his own production company, as you know. Ambition is a heady mistress. I can't fight it. You remember it didn't work with Larry, and it won't work now."

Morris peered closely at her. "Baloney. You're a big girl, honey, and you know your own mind, even though I think your reasoning is off base. Larry wasn't worth it. Zack is."

Morris tossed his empty soda can into the wastebasket, changing the topic to ease Hannah's distress. "You're going to enjoy the picnic. We do it every year. It's a way to say a small thank you for all the hours everyone puts in. You can come in jeans, but I want you to dress Sarah in her finest togs. I want to show my niece off."

Hannah got up to leave, then paused. "Morris," she said quietly. "I'd like to get back to what you said about fighting for a man if he's worth having."

"Yes?"

"It works both ways."

Hannah dressed Sarah like royalty, not because Morris had asked her, but because she had no choice. Zack purchased Sarah's outfit, a baby Dior, for an outrageous price and refused to let her reimburse him.

"Discretion is the better part of valor, Hannah." He reached into another shopping bag and took out two stuffed animals. Hannah was used to scrimping and saving. Zack's generosity overwhelmed her and saddened her. It was as if he were using material goods to make up for the words she longed to hear.

Her heart burst with pride when she saw her daughter all dressed up. Sarah was a little princess in a lavender dress with rows of ruffles and anklets to match, her tuft of baby-fine hair twirled together with a tiny lavender clip, decorated with hearts. Pinned to her chest was another heart with her name written on it.

To the oohing and aahing of the crew from WBC, Sarah was passed around from person to person. Her eyes wide with excitement, she was on her best behavior, with a smile for everyone. But her best dimpled smile was saved for Zack, who timed each person's brief handling of her as he warned them sternly not to kiss her.

"I don't hold with that. You might have something." Then he sucked on her fingers and kissed her. So much for fairness. Hannah giggled and lifted her shoulders, as if to tell the startled onlookers Zack was nuts.

The weather was mail-order perfect. Bright blue sky, ribbons of wisping clouds, a soft breeze to cool off the picnickers as they played games or sat around eating. Morris had rented a tent with flags flying from the tops of the supporting posts. There was a carnival atmosphere that everyone enjoyed. Games and food were provided for all. Hot dogs, hamburgers, and, for the cholesterol-conscious, chicken. Musical machines spun sugar candy. A strolling magician and a clown entertained the children. An area was set aside for games of skill.

"They're rigged," Zack said.

"You can beat them," Hannah replied.

"You're right." He handed her the baby.

Hannah held Sarah while Zack tossed wooden rings onto pegs. "What do I get if we win?" she asked, cheering him on when he had only one more to toss.

She found out soon enough, as the masked man operating the ring toss handed her a bag of lollipops. "Scott, you devil," she exclaimed as he removed the mask. "I can get this anytime." She strolled off hugging a doll, which Zack immediately confiscated to give to Sarah. She was having fun, and if Zack was soon going to leave she wasn't going to think about it today. Today was for memories.

They paused to watch a game of horseshoes. Sarah

clapped her hands and kicked her little feet, catching one of the contestant's eye. Johnny, a cameraman, tossed the winning shoe, then came over to them.

The father of five held out his arms. "She's a honey. Give her here a sec."

Zack saw the dust on his arms and hands and clothes, the sweat on his face. "Maybe later. Sarah needs to get out of the sun."

"It's shady right here," Hannah said, following as Zack strode away. "You hurt his feelings."

Zack stared down at her. A slow flush crept up his neck. "He was dirty."

Hannah exploded with laughter. And that was how it went. Zack unceremoniously swung Sarah out of the way of anyone he didn't want touching her, while she gurgled and laughed, thinking it was a new game.

The women who'd placed bets on Heartthrob and fantasized about making love with him saw the way he looked at Hannah and "protected" her baby from germs. Each experienced a moment of regret, then they whispered to one another, pausing to smile, for who could be angry in the face of such adoration. Within the hour Heartthrob was taken out of the betting pool. All monies were returned by Betsie, the treasurer for that sort of thing. A new bet was placed on Scott.

Blissfully unaware of the show they were putting on, Hannah told Zack he was too fussy. "A little dirt can't harm her." His brows knit in displeasure as he chastised her.

"Really, Hannah. There's dirt and there's dirt."

She marveled at this giant of a teddy bear who was ready to ward off all threats to her daughter—including a little honest dust. How could she not love him?

The sun had gone down by the time they returned home with an exhausted and now cranky Sarah. She let the two adults know show time was over. "Here, I'll bathe her," Zack said.

"Uh, uh. Not this time. What she wants you don't have. Go fix us something to drink."

Zack stayed in the kitchen instead of going in while Hannah nursed Sarah. He had an unpleasant task to perform. Telling her he was leaving next week wasn't going to be easy. He'd turn the making of the environment documentary over to Scott. Morris already knew and was genuinely sad to see him go. "Maybe you'll be back sooner than you think, Zack," he said.

Thinking of Hannah, Zack wished it were true, but Carl had found a new studio. The Denver documentary wouldn't take long to shoot, since all the information and the sets were in a museum in Denver. But then there were other job possibilities Carl had spoken of.

He waited until Sarah was bathed, fed, and put to bed, then came up to Hannah and put his arms around her. "Hannah, I didn't want this news to be a repeat of the other time. Carl's found a place and he's lined up people for me to interview." He saw the effect his words had on her, saw her begin to distance herself from him. "Hey, it's not going to be forever."

She freed herself. "Of course not," she said, knowing it would be an eternity. He left three days later.

• • •

Zack's sudden departure left a hole in Hannah's life. She found herself dashing into his office to tell him something or to discuss an idea for a show, only to be confronted by an empty desk and chair. In the evening she tried to put him out of her mind, but failed completely. Instead she clung to Sarah more, talking about Zack as if he were still there. She hadn't been able to say good-bye to him; it was the way they'd both wanted it.

With a heavy heart she went about her tasks, busy with preparations for the follow-up environment show, which Scott directed. Before he left, Zack had discussed with Scott the plans for the show, including the appearance of the Governor.

A week after Zack left, Madge, who was recuperating at home, sent word she was ready to receive visitors. Hannah went during lunch that same day. She'd been waiting anxiously to see Madge. She arrived at the long rambling ranch house in the foothills of the Watchung Mountains with a bouquet of daisies. Madge's devoted husband, Bill, ushered her onto a sun porch, dotted with green and white wicker furniture. Madge lay on a chaise, her legs covered with an afghan.

"Bill makes too much of a fuss over me," she groused, but her eyes were twinkling, letting Hannah know she really loved it.

Hannah smiled, bending down to kiss her friend. "You're looking good, Madge."

Madge patted her arm. "Let's take a look at you, up close and personal, that is." She smiled. "I already know how you look on camera, Hannah—

nothing short of terrific. What you've done with the show these past couple of weeks is wonderful. Keep up the good work."

Hannah pooh-poohed her. "I'm not doing anything but holding down the fort, Madge. We can't wait to see you back on the job." She pulled up a chair and covertly studied her friend. She'd expected Madge to look better. She'd lost weight. The veins stuck out on her neck and her coloring was quite pale. She'd had an allergic reaction to one of the medicines, and it was clear she would need a long recuperation period.

"How's that sweet baby of yours?" Madge asked.

"She's fine."

"And her mother?"

"She's fine too."

Madge's probing look roamed her face. "Liar."

Hannah shrugged. "All right. Almost fine." She smiled.

Madge adjusted the pillow behind her head. "Do you want to talk about it? Zack left earlier than expected. I understand Scott's helping you with your show—"

"*Your* show, Madge," Hannah interrupted. She didn't want her to think she had designs on the show.

Madge lifted her hand, then let it flop down on her lap. "It's yours while you're at the helm. Hand me that glass of water, please."

While Madge slowly drank the water, Hannah glanced out the window at the sloping yard. She felt as though she were in a clearing in a forest. Tall elms and maples bordered the neatly mown lawn.

"That looks like fun," Hannah said, eyeing the redwood swing.

"Bring Sarah over and enjoy it. Now tell me about you and Zack."

Hannah settled back in her chair. "There's nothing to say. He phoned last night and said he's getting settled into an apartment. Denver is nice. Carl's got things lined up and he begins interviewing tomorrow."

"How long will he be gone?"

"I don't know. From there he might be going out West."

Madge frowned. "Is he coming back for a visit?"

"When he can." She looked away, then added quietly, "I doubt it." Her voice was filled with pain. "There's really no reason. What we had was an interlude. It's better this way. Neither of us will get hurt."

"That's a crock!" Madge said.

Hannah silently agreed with her.

Ten

Zack leaned against his Jeep, gazing at the soaring peaks of the Rocky Mountains. He wished they were the Watchung Mountains instead and that Hannah and Sarah were with him. He'd driven up to the Continental Divide and Twin Lakes after meeting with the historians, who were helping him understand the area better. If Hannah were there he could show her the wagon-wheel tracks made by settlers on their trek west, so fragile was the topsoil in parts of Denver. She would be fascinated by the sweep and grandeur of the area.

But only if she could forgive him for not writing or calling in three weeks. Which he doubted. Nor did he blame her. He'd wanted to see what life would be like totally on his own, without worrying about anyone but himself.

The fact was he hated it. He missed Hannah terribly, and Sarah too. And then there was the phone call from Madge two nights ago.

"You're a jerk, Zack!" she'd said in her usual blunt manner. "What's more, you don't deserve a woman like Hannah."

He knew that.

"Furthermore," Madge had gone on, "I've invited Nat Edwards to my home a week from Sunday. He's thrilled, and particularly asked that Hannah be invited, if at all possible. So, big shot, put that in your Indian pipe and smoke it!"

Scott's tone wasn't much better the first few times they'd talked. They'd kept in touch, ostensibly to discuss Scott's work on Hannah's follow-up show. Scott was cool, almost to the point of letting Zack know he was persona non grata. "Hannah's doing well," he'd said the day before. "My guess is she'll make quite a name for herself as an investigative reporter, but I guess you're not really interested in hearing about her."

He was. Desperately.

Carl appeared on the trail, distracting Zack from his miserable thoughts. Carl was a big man, with red hair, a shaggy beard, and muscles twice the size of Zack's. He could have been one of the mountain men who'd settled in the area, climbed Pikes Peak, built a log cabin, and hunted for food. He strode up to Zack, a video cam on his shoulder. "The area's pretty rough down there, but I think we'll be able to bring our equipment in. As soon as the script is finalized we'll hire a local to do the voice-over."

Zack nodded. He didn't much care who Carl hired; he just wanted to get on with it. What used to be a joy was turning into a chore. "How long do you figure, Carl?"

Carl had a way of looking at a person, knowing his inner thoughts. "What's wrong, pal?"

Zack threw down the blade of grass he was chewing on. "Nothing's wrong."

"You seem in quite a hurry to get through with this. I thought you enjoyed roughing it, being free, doing whatever you pleased."

"I thought so too. It doesn't matter." Zack piled his notebooks back into the Jeep, then hoisted himself up onto the seat. "Come on. Let's head back."

Carl put the video cam in the backseat. His hiking boots were covered with dust. Zack remembered how Hannah had laughed at him when he wouldn't let someone hold Sarah, because his hands were dusty. Lord, he'd give a lot to hear her laugh right now.

"Your old boss called this morning," Carl said. "I meant to tell you before."

Zack's head whipped around, a troubled frown knitting his brow. If Morris was calling, it might mean Hannah or the baby was in trouble. "What did he say? Is everything all right at home?"

"I expect so," Carl said casually. "Maybe he called just to say hello."

Zack doubted it. Morris never did anything without a plan. He couldn't begin to guess what it was, though.

Carl had rented space at a local television station. Zack parked the Jeep in the lot and they strode inside. Soon they were watching the film in the editing suite. Before they were finished, Carl would shoot six hours' worth of film, to be edited down to an hour. Zack had almost finished writing the script.

"It looks okay to me," Carl said. "What about you?"

"It's all right, but I think you need to get inside the museum too. There's a wealth of history there that can be related to the actual location shots." What had Morris called for? "Listen, I'll be back in a little while. I'm calling home."

Carl stared at him. "Go right ahead."

Zack dialed Morris, only to be informed that he had left town for a few days. "Where can I reach him?"

"You can't," Florence, his secretary, said. "Morris is traveling."

"Doesn't he call in?" Dammit, he should in case Hannah needed him.

"Zack," Florence said, sounding testy, "Morris is not a doctor. He doesn't have to phone in."

"What if his family needs him?" he barked, threading his fingers through his hair. Never had he been so frustrated. Sarah might get sick—then what?

"By 'family,' " Florence said, "I take it you mean Hannah. Mr. Edwards is in town. Either he or Scott will be glad to offer their services. We all think the world of Hannah. Have a nice day, Zack. Good-bye."

He stared at the receiver.

"How are things at home?" Carl asked as Zack sat down hard in his chair. His foot tapped at a furious rate. He mumbled under his breath. "Zack?"

"Huh?"

"I asked how things are at home. Why did Morris call?"

"How the hell should I know? Morris left town."

"Buddy, I don't know what you're so angry about, but whatever it is, you're in no condition to work. Your mind is somewhere else, and unless I miss my guess there's a woman causing this unhappiness."

Zack scowled, saying nothing. Pushing himself out of the chair, he paced the floor.

"That won't solve anything, Zack."

"It's too late. I let her get away. She means everything in the world to me, and I blew it. Now there's another man on the scene—Nat Edwards—and here I am."

"Whew! That's some heavy-duty competition, pal. If I were you I'd take the next plane out of here and drag her back if necessary."

"That's just it. For reasons I don't care to go into, Hannah needs a home. She needs to walk up the path, open the door, and see familiar things."

Carl raised his brows. "You mean if she loves you she won't move?"

"We never spoke of love."

Carl shook his head. "Buddy, you're in worse shape than I thought." He stood up, towering over his friend. "Zack, you've got two choices. Either I throw you out of here, or . . ."

Zack grinned. "Yes?"

Carl slapped his shoulder. "I throw you out of here. Go home and straighten out your life."

Zack kissed his cheek. Carl glowered at him.

Morris glowered at Carl that evening. "You what! I flew halfway across the country to knock some sense into that young man's head and you beat me to it."

Carl eased himself out of his chair. Morris gulped. "How about a drink, Morris?"

Zack rang Hannah's bell. He was almost afraid she might not be alone. He was in no mood to deal with Nat Edwards, but if he had to he'd throw him out.

Hannah opened the door, carrying Sarah on her shoulder. Speechless, she automatically delivered the infant into Zack's outstretched arms.

"Are you here for a visit, Zack?" she asked formally. She'd spent too many nights dreaming up what she'd say. Her voice sounded tinny, stilted.

He was nervous. Hannah looked like an angel in jeans and an old T-shirt. He'd teased her about it once because it had kept falling off one shoulder, giving him a place to kiss. She unconsciously pushed it back into place.

"I missed you," he said. "I missed both of you."

"Funny. I'd never have known it. If you're looking for Morris, he isn't here."

He hitched his foot on the top step. He hadn't felt so nervous since high school. "I wasn't looking for Morris. I came because of you. May I come in?"

"Really?" She tossed her hair over her shoulder, gazing at him directly. "As you can see, we're both fine. Peachy, actually. Madge isn't due back for another three months. She plans on carrying a light schedule. Nat has been here. Too bad you missed him."

"I know he's been here and I'm glad I missed him."

Hannah was surprised. "You know?"

"Madge called me. She read me the riot act, and she was right."

Hannah moved to the side, giving Zack permission to enter her house. "I have no idea why she would do that. Anyway, it doesn't matter. I'm thriving."

"Well, I'm not."

"See a doctor then."

He put Sarah in her playpen. They stood like antagonists on either side of it. "I'm in love with Sarah."

A smile tugged at Hannah's lips. "So am I," she said softly.

"I'm also in love with her mother." His gaze held hers, preventing her from turning away. Slowly he walked over to her. "I love you, Hannah. I have from the first, but was too afraid to tell you."

"What does that mean?" she asked, picking up the scent she knew so well. She longed to feel his arms going around her, yet drew away.

For a terrible, horrible instant, he thought she would refuse him, push him away. "It means," he said, "that if you don't consent to marry me I'm going into that playpen with Sarah and never coming out."

His lips nipped at her mouth, his tongue urged it open. With a sigh she reached up to twine her arms around his neck, kissing him back with all the longing she'd felt the last few weeks.

They stayed like that for a long time, renewing their desire, making a pledge with their bodies. "Say it," he whispered, his eyes boring into hers. "Say it."

"I love you," she said. "I love you with all my heart."

"And I don't have to live in the playpen?" he teased.

"How about a different-size playpen?"

"Hannah," he said, when he released her again. "I want to adopt Sarah. She's mine in my heart. I want her to have my name so that when our other children are born, she won't feel slighted. I love you and her."

Hannah laid her cheek on his chest, feeling the beating of his heart.

That was how Morris found them.

"So here you are!" he stormed. "I'm sick and tired of solving your problems. Why didn't you stay in Denver?"

Hannah and Zack continued to hold each other. "Morris," Hannah said, "we're perfectly capable of solving our own problems. Zack's asked me to marry him, and I've accepted."

"What about staying in one place?"

"I found out you were right. Where Zack is, is home."

"Beautiful speech. Now listen to mine. I tried it out on Carl first. He thinks it's a terrific idea." He pushed a stunned Zack and Hannah onto the sofa, ordering them not to interrupt.

"I've got a yen to get back to my first love. Hannah, you knew that. Zack, I purposely picked you as my successor, but you're such a stubborn mule you always fought me tooth and nail."

Zack started to rise. "Now see here—"

"Don't interrupt! You want to make your documentaries and I want to do what I do best. For that I realize we both need a free hand. You also don't have a home base with the proper equipment. From what Carl tells me, you're so moonstruck that you'll probably want to stick around and direct your wife and watch the kiddies grow. So what do you say? Will you move your base of operations back here? You can have a free hand. Carl thinks it's a great idea. He's convinced that you're no good to him otherwise."

Zack was speechless. When Hannah threw her arms around him, kissing him on the mouth, he realized he'd found the perfect voice-over for his documentary, the perfect solution to all his dreams. She was in his arms, where she belonged.

He responded immediately. "Morris, you've got a deal."

"And you, son, have a telegram. It came yesterday."

Hannah watched eagerly as he ripped it open. The smile that spread over his face clutched at her heart. "What is it?"

"Honey, how would you like to be married to a man who just won an ACE Award? We can combine going to the ceremony with a honeymoon."

"Congratulations," Morris said, but they weren't paying any attention to him. The way those two were smothering each other was embarrassing.

"Come on, Sarah." He lifted his great-niece from the playpen. "You're too young for this. Let's go call Alex and Madge. We have a wedding to plan, and you're going to be the flower girl."